A BRIDGE ABRIDGED

A Bridge Abridged

A short story collection
by

STEPHEN GALLAS

Adelaide Books
New York / Lisbon
2019

A BRIDGE ABRIDGED
A short story collection
By Stephen Gallas

Published by Adelaide Books, New York / Lisbon
adelaidebooks.org

Editor-in-Chief
Stevan V. Nikolic

For any information, please address Adelaide Books
at info@adelaidebooks.org

or write to:

Adelaide Books
244 Fifth Ave. Suite D27
New York, NY, 10001

ISBN: 978-1-951896-00-3

Printed in the United States of America

To Jungeun, my travel partner.

Contents

Noraebang Night Shift

Muffled music emanated from the walls of Room 6. Hyun-ok scrolled through old pictures on her phone. In one of the pictures, on a trip out into the hills of Gapyeong, Hyun-ok and her husband were standing knee-deep in the river, holding their young daughter So-yeon above the water, each hand gripped by a different parent. Back then the family was carefree. Sure, the karaoke business was keeping them busy, as their noraebang was in one of the busier neighborhoods, but they were happy with that. So-yeon had been just three years old on that trip to Gapyeong, and Hyun-ok herself hadn't yet been old enough for people on the street to call her "ahjumma." Now she'd reached the age at which people spoke to her like the motherly figure she was. She looked the same way that most matronly women who were called "ahjumma" looked, with her short black hair teased into a sort of afro and her clothes typically being of the open-air market variety.

A pair of businessmen were in Room 6, belting "Nest" by Namjin. Singing the songs of an old time pop legend was the best way to cap off a night of soju and barbecue. These kinds of guys were common customers in the noraebang. It was the only room occupied in her place at the moment, as it was roughly 2:30 a.m. This being Sinchon, one of the liveliest neighborhoods in Seoul, the late night crowd would probably begin to pour in pretty soon, and Hyun-ok needed to take advantage of the situation and make sure that the place was ready for the surge.

The refrigerator behind her was full of beer, soju, soda, and water, so that was ready to go. Hyun-ok checked all of the karaoke rooms and made sure that they were devoid of used glasses and plates, and that they all had their remote controls and song binders in place. No karaoke without the ability to pick songs, after all. Hyun-ok would definitely need snacks for her customers, because drinking was senseless without snacks so she went back into the kitchen to double check. The kitchen was small but had a refrigerator, shelves, a sink, a cutting board, and all of the necessary cutlery for preparing food. Next to the refrigerator was a mattress, which Hyun-ok sometimes slept on during weekday night shifts, but never on the weekends.

In going through the refrigerator and shelves, Hyun-ok confirmed that she had a sufficient amount of watermelon, Korean melon, bananas, dried squid, and pretzels to get her through the evening. Last but not least, she had four huge bags of gangnaengi in her arsenal. The sweet popcorn was the perfect complement to karaoke. The only thing that went better with this popcorn was dongdongju, but Hyun-ok had stopped selling all types of rice wine awhile ago.

Customers only wanted to drink beer and soju these days. As for the unisex bathroom, Hyun-ok had recently bought soap, so she assumed that it was fine.

This late at night, the noraebang seemed to be a lot more dismal than in the earlier hours.

There were no windows, so the red glow from the ceiling was the only source of light, and red lights could make even charity work seem like an illicit affair. Even without the red lights, Hyun-ok felt like she was sneaking around, despite there being nothing wrong with karaoke.

Perhaps it was because her husband had never liked her being away from home at this hour. Unlike the other men in the neighborhood, Hyun-ok's husband did not like to play bumper pool and drink soju until he was blind, initially. With costs for So-yeon's education mounting, however, he began working late and going on more drinking outings with his coworkers. He hadn't been as absent in the past, and actually talked plenty about how he enjoyed coming home to watch TV with his family, but that wasn't the way things were while their marriage was fraying. Laughs grew infrequent, and fights increased.

Hyun-ok's decision to fire the night shift employee and start working the shift herself did not sit well with her husband, and this was the fight that changed the makeup of the family.

According to his line of reasoning, she should have closed the noraebang if she couldn't afford to staff it. They argued over Hyun-ok's determination to keep that extra source of income, and now she was working the night shift out of necessity.

Their mothers had known each other from a calligraphy class back in Ulsan, and upon realizing they had a son and daughter of roughly the same age, set the two of them up. Hyun-ok, back then young and pretty, happily obeyed her mother. Now, she wished she'd been more rebellious.

The idea that she shouldn't make sacrifices in order to benefit her family still nagged at her. What was the point of lambasting her work ethic? In the modern age, making sacrifices was the only way to tread water. Resounding success generally meant playing politics, and that route was littered with the trampled remains of old opponents.

As Hyun-ok braced herself for the late wave, she received a message from So-yeon. It read, "Are you coming home tonight?"

She responded with, "Yes." Then she winced and typed, "Did you do your homework?"

So-yeon answered, "I started it but couldn't finish it. It was too hard to write the sentences."

Hyun-ok started to type a reproach, but deleted it. Instead, she wrote, "Go to sleep, my So-yeon. You can write them tomorrow."

A group of five young men, most likely students at Yonsei University, came in. They were laughing and teasing each other about how they struck out with girls at the bar they had just been at. Hyun-ok smiled, processed their payment for one hour of songs, and led them to Room 4. Red, pleather, cushioned sofas hugged the back and side walls, and a table stood within reach of the seating. The big screen TV was the strongest source of light in the room, which was otherwise mottled with specks of blue and green light. Hyun-ok indicated that if the students needed anything from her such as beer or snacks, they could press the call button attached squarely to the table. The boys told her they understood, and one of them picked up the karaoke remote and put on "Fantastic Baby" by Big Bang. All of the boys started jumping up and down, and fought over the two microphones as Hyun-ok exited the room.

When she got back to the front desk, a young couple who probably also attended Yonsei University was standing there. They held each other's hands lightly below the counter, and Hyun-ok received their payment for one hour's worth of karaoke. She led the couple to Room 9, which looked a lot like Rooms 4 and 6 but smaller, and walked back to the desk. She heard music start, but no singing. It was at moments like this that she wondered why young people couldn't just have sex elsewhere, because she didn't feel like dealing with it. She was also happy that the couches in her noraebang were pleather.

It wasn't as if she needed much of a reason to do so, but Hyun-ok thought of So-yeon any time she saw students from Yonsei University. So-yeon had recently enrolled at an after school English academy in order to keep up with everyone else. The girl was only ten years old, but having never studied English up to this point meant that she was behind her peers. At the academy, her classmates were second graders, and other kids of her age and level were deemed to be dimwitted. While Hyun-ok hated that she had to pay as much as she had to in order to send her daughter to a place to study as opposed to play or draw, she knew that she had no real choice.

With any luck and the proper preparation, So-yeon might one day attend the same school as all of these drunken customers singing karaoke like it was their last night on Earth.

The businessmen shuffled out of Room 6, with their shoes sticking to the floor, and thanked Hyun-ok for her business. One of them wore thick black-rimmed frames that looked silly, because that trend was common among people much younger than he was. She wished them a good night, and thanked them for coming in. Once they were gone, she went into the room for the cleanup effort. One of the beer bottles lay in a puddle, and it did not appear as if the men had made any effort to clean it up. Hyun-ok handled the mess, collected all of the rest of the glasses and bottles, and made her way back to the counter.

Once she was there, she saw that a new message had come in from So-yeon. It read, "But I can't sleep."

"Why not?"

"It's hard for me to sleep when you're not here."

Hyun-ok sighed and typed, "I know. You found the food in the refrigerator, right?"

"Yes."

"Good. Now go to sleep, my baby." So-yeon did not immediately respond.

A rabble of English resounded in the stairwell, and Hyun-ok knew that some difficulty was afoot. She didn't speak any English, which meant that handling the transaction of these potential customers would be a lot more tedious than it had been for the other customers. She was happy that she had her calculator with her at the counter, because that way she could display the price. Hyun-ok didn't particularly like foreigners, mostly because they typically refused to learn Korean and showed no real regard for anything around them. She guessed that she was going to have to walk them through the process of selecting a song, turning on the microphone, and ordering snacks. On one previous occasion, a group of foreigners had pressed the call button, and when she went into their room to take their order, they were surprised to see her. They had evidently not known what the call button was, and pressed it out of sheer curiosity. Then they laughed at her like it had been her fault. In the present moment, Hyun-ok hoped that someone among the group knew how to speak Korean, or that a Korean was among them.

The foreigners cascaded down the stairs and flooded into the noraebang. Hyun-ok counted six among them, with none of them being Korean. Four of the foreigners were male, and two of them were female. Everyone looked to be in their early to mid twenties. One of the women, a blonde one, approached the counter and held up two fingers. Hyun-ok guessed that this meant two hours, so she typed in "60000" on her calculator and showed it to the customer. She was transfixed by the foreigner's green eyes, because she had never seen anyone with that eye color before. It looked alien. The blonde turned away from Hyun-ok and said something to the group. It took a moment to figure out that the figure represented 60,000 won and that after converting it, the price wasn't too bad. They seemed to come to an agreement, as they all nodded and did not protest, so Hyun-ok led the group to Room 10.

The foreigners were enjoying themselves. As soon as they arrived in the room, one of the men grabbed the tambourine and started banging it against his hand. He hadn't any semblance of rhythm. One of the foreign girls, who was shorter and had curly black hair, tried to wrest the tambourine away from him. The whole display was way too loud and annoying for Hyun-ok, so she quickly handed the song binder to the green-eyed girl and left the room without explaining how to select songs. It's not like they would have understood, anyway. The only sound to come out of the room as she walked away was group chatter, and only after a few minutes did "Gangnam Style" start throbbing through the walls. Even though it had been a year since that song had become world-famous, it was still playing everywhere in Seoul. Hyun-ok now knew every word of it, but in her head she never heard it as sung by PSY. She only heard the cracking, tone deaf attempts of her customers.

She walked past Room 9. Music was still playing, but nobody was singing.

She walked past Room 4. One of the boys was singing "I Am the Best" by 2NE1, and he was struggling to keep pace with CL's rapping.

She figured that if she was going to have to watch over three rooms with a total of thirteen people, she might as well eat something. So she stopped in the kitchen and grabbed herself some dried squid, because that was her favorite snack. As Hyun-ok bit her first piece of squid, she saw another message from So-yeon.

It read, "Can I keep the lights in your room on?" Hyun-ok typed, "If it helps you go to sleep, yes."

"Mom."

"Yes?"

"My friends at the academy said that I'll never get into Yonsei, and that I'll have to go to Seogang."

Hyun-ok sighed. Seogang University was not nearly as prestigious as Yonsei, and no employer would take So-yeon seriously if she approached them with a Seogang degree in hand. "Don't worry, you'll go to Yonsei," Hyun-ok responded. "And we shouldn't even be talking about this right now. You should be sleeping." After that message, Hyun-ok sent an emoticon of a dog falling asleep.

The bell rang, indicating that Room 10 had pressed the call button. Maybe these foreigners had done it by mistake, too.

When Hyun-ok went into the room, a wave of American rap washed over her, and the tambourine guy was mumbling nonsensically. Whatever he was dribbling off key was playing over with the curly-haired girl, as she was singing along with him. The blonde ordered beer and soju, and held up her fingers to indicate the amount of bottles. Three big bottles of beer, and two bottles of soju. The other members of the group were relaxing on the pleather seating, shouting away. Hyun-ok cringed, because the noise hurt her ears.

As she left the room, a thought came over her — these people, who spent their nights drinking and singing, were most likely the type of people teaching English to So-yeon at the language academy. Hyun-ok agreed that young people should have fun, but she wondered if these people realized what they held in their hands every day they went to work. They spent their time drinking until dawn, as if they were on a prolonged vacation. Did they know that So-yeon's future depended on the development of her English, and that she would never be able to work the kind of job she wanted if she failed to catch up to and surpass her peers? Did the teachers know that So-yeon's progression hinged on their performance? Maybe the other mothers in the neighborhood assumed the teachers to be effective simply because of English being their mother tongue, but how many of these teachers were formally trained in teaching children? It was clear to Hyun-ok that they, with the exception of the blonde one, did not care the least bit about the education of their students. The problem with these English academies was that the vast majority of teachers did not care. Hiring a tutor was an option that often yielded better results, but that was too expensive of an option for Hyun-ok.

Back at the front desk, another coed group of friends waited, but they were neither students nor foreign. If Hyun-ok had to guess, she would say that the group was in their thirties. Apparently staying out this late wasn't only for young people. The group was professional throughout the transaction. Hyun-ok led them to Room 5, and that was that. When she listened to them through the walls, however, she heard one of the men in the group make a squealing attempt at "Somebody That I Used to Know" by Gotye. One of the women contributed a serviceable attempt and salvaged the performance somewhat.

That was the last group of customers to walk through the door, so all Hyun-ok had to do now was wait until everyone's time was up. She noticed that So-yeon hadn't responded to her latest text. Maybe she had finally fallen asleep. With the competing melodies and voices pumping through the norae-bang, Hyun-ok killed time by playing Angry Birds.

When she was on the verge of setting a new high score, Hyun-ok heard one of the doors shut. She looked down the hall and saw one of the foreigners approaching. It was the tambourine player.

He arrived at the desk and instantly exuded an air disagreeable to Hyun-ok. He smiled at her, and she tried to make sense of what he wanted as she stared into his dead, drunken eyes.

Assuming he had to go to the bathroom, Hyun-ok pointed the other way and said, "Toilet," in English.

That didn't seem to register with the foreigner, as he continued to leer at Hyun-ok. "Toilet," she pointed and repeated.

After three full seconds, the foreigner turned and ascertained the position of the bathroom.

Hyun-ok nodded and said, "Yes."

The foreigner giggled and began to walk to the bathroom. As he left the lobby, he attempted to say, "I love you," in Korean. He slurred it too much for Hyun-ok to be able to understand it.

He meandered down the hall, scraping against the walls, and bobbed his head to the music. Hyun-ok noted the time he arrived in the bathroom as 3:30. She went back to playing Angry Birds.

At 3:35, the group of male students filed out of Room 4, their hour having expired.

Hyun-ok thanked them for their business on their way out, keeping an eye on whether or not they were too drunk. She went into the room and found that they had smuggled in Cass beer, apparently afraid that Hyun-ok wouldn't sell them beer because of their age. This struck her as odd, because if they were university students, they would have been of age.

Maybe the outside Cass was simply cheaper than what she sold at the noraebang. Either way, it didn't please Hyun-ok, and she resolved to adopt a harder line on future beer smugglings.

She finished the Room 4 cleanup at 3:40, and saw that the door to Room 9 was wide open. The couple in there must have simply left when their time expired. Hyun-ok checked and saw that this was the case, and smelled the postcoital musk lingering in the air. She would have to grab some Lysol from the bathroom and spray down the couches. It was possible that she would even have to mop the floor. Better safe than sorry.

The foreigners in Room 10 were singing "Hey Jude," which was a song Hyun-ok knew well. She used to sing it with her husband in the time when they'd been able to use the bar for their own enjoyment. Room 5 was too far away for her to hear what the customers in there were singing, but it seemed that they were still having a good time. Now that there were only two occupied rooms in the noraebang, Hyun-ok felt at ease. While walking down the dark hallway, she inhaled deeply through her nose and thought that her most difficult task remaining was to wipe down Room 9. After that she could simply sit at her desk and play her game some more. Maybe she would even find a way to beat her high score.

When she arrived at the bathroom, however, Hyun-ok found that the door was locked.

She tried twisting the knob again, but it did not yield. She knocked and waited for a response, but the occupant was silent. The door was not of the best quality, however, and Hyun-ok knew how to work it open even if it was locked. She twisted the knob about thirty degrees to the left, turned it about ten degrees to the right, then quickly turned it all the way to the left. The lock clicked, and Hyun-ok had access to the restroom.

To Hyun-ok's surprise, the door opened only partially, because it was blocked by someone lying on the floor. It was the drunken foreigner. She tried to call out to him, but he did not respond. She even tried to bang the door on his curled up legs, but the result was the same.

Hyun-ok put all of her force into pushing the door open, and after a few spirited attempts, she was finally able to work it open enough for her to slide into the room.

Upon entering the bathroom, the stench of bile overcame her. The foreigner had thrown up, with the majority of the vomit lying in a puddle on the floor. He was laying his head in it. Hyun-ok shook him by the shoulders. It took a series of shakes — and Hyun-ok thinking that she had broken his collarbone — for him to wake up. Once he did, he called out what was presumably a girl's name. Hyun-ok went back to Room 10 to get somebody.

Hyun-ok interrupted Sisqo's "Thong Song" and beckoned for the blonde foreigner to come with her. Upon seeing what was happening, the curly-headed one volunteered to accompany Hyun-ok to the bathroom. The blonde one stayed behind, but watched the two women leave.

Hyun-ok showed the curly-headed girl the drunken man on the bathroom floor. When he saw that Hyun-ok had brought her, he shook his head and emitted a guttural groan. The curly-headed girl attempted to assure Hyun-ok that the young man would be fine, but Hyun-ok ran and got the blonde girl.

What transpired between the two women when the blonde arrived was most certainly a terse exchange. Hyun-ok did not know what they were saying, but that didn't mean that she was unable to pick up on nonverbal clues. She guessed that they were bickering over who should take care of the pile of human on her bathroom floor, and she admittedly enjoyed the exchange. It was settled that the blonde, green-eyed foreigner would be taking care of the guy, and Hyun-ok was all the more thankful for the episode being over. She was also happy that the blonde one was the one who was going to be helping out. If any of these foreigners could help the drunk guy, it was her. She seemed to Hyun-ok to be observant and caring. The other girl simply came off as needy and narcissistic. Hyun-ok hadn't observed the other people in the group too much, but she assumed that they were selfish and didn't want their good time to be dampered. They hadn't made any effort to help their friend. Maybe they weren't friends at all.

After a forceful effort of coercion and sweet talk from the blonde, the young man made it onto his feet. Hyun-ok called a taxi and, alongside the blonde, helped carry him up the stairs and out of the noraebang.

After the couple was out of sight, the rest of the night was easy. She wouldn't have admitted it, but Hyun-ok had temporarily fallen asleep at the counter. When everyone was gone, she decided that it was time to close the noraebang for the night. It was nearing 5 a.m.

The streets of Sinchon at this time were like a post-apocalyptic nightmare. Hyun-ok couldn't help but think that a horde of zombies had just fanned out over the neighborhood, leaving beer cans, styrofoam bowls, and other trash along the way. The street food stalls, teeming in the night, were left shuttered and abandoned. Some of the zombies remained in the streets, swaying with every step and leaning on each other for support. Hyun-ok could safely assume that these people were not the church-going type, because zombies didn't attend church, especially if they had spent the previous night on the prowl. Despite the setting being made even more dismal by the muted sunlight failing to work its way past the office buildings, Hyun-ok knew that the neighborhood would look as clean and cosmopolitan as ever within just a few hours. Seoul was regenerative like that.

Craving something to eat, Hyun-ok stepped into an alley restaurant because it was the only one open at this time. She scarfed down a tuna kimbap and sympathized with other ah-jummas who, like her, had to work while their families rested at home. She left as little of a mess as she possibly could during her quick meal, and made her way out as fast as she could.

The buildings of the neighborhood loomed over Hyun-ok as she emerged from the labyrinth of the back streets. If she kept walking straight for a bit, she would end up home. If she went straight even further still, she would reach the Han River. Hyun-ok knew that it would be beautiful in the morning light, but there was no way that she was going to go to the river instead of home to her daughter.

As she navigated the sidewalk around the intersection, Hyun-ok noticed a man in a suit sleeping on a ledge. When she got closer, she saw that he had thick, black-rimmed glasses lying on the ground next to him. It was the same businessman who had been in her noraebang singing "Nest" a few hours earlier. She considered prodding the man awake and telling him that he needed to go home, but thought twice before doing so. She had already roused one drunk man awake in the past hour; it wasn't her responsibility to do it again. Besides, if the man had not been robbed by this point, it was highly unlikely that he was going to get robbed at all. Maybe, just maybe, he preferred sleeping on concrete ledges. There was no way for Hyun-ok to know.

As Hyun-ok proceeded home, the sun shot through a slit between two buildings and caught her in the eye. After squinting and holding her hand up to block the light, she saw

Seogang University across the street. It was a small, unassuming university, nestled between the high rise apartments like an egg between the twigs of a nest. Before Hyun-ok could think any further about her disdain for any university not named Yonsei, her phone vibrated in her pocket.

Hyun-ok dug the pulsing monolith out of her pocket and read the caller ID. The call was from So-yeon. Hyun-ok stopped in her tracks and answered the call.

"So-yeon?"

"Mom." Her daughter's voice sounded stable, but that didn't stop Hyun-ok from worrying.

"Did you ever fall asleep?"

"I did, but then I woke up and you weren't here."

"I'll be home soon," Hyun-ok said as she continued to shield her eyes from the sun.

"I don't like waking up without you here, mommy. I don't like the noraebang," So-yeon said, her voice quavering.

"I've had the noraebang since before you were born, honey. It's always fun to have your own place to sing songs, isn't it?"

"Why do we need a place to sing songs? Can't we just sing anywhere?"

Hyun-ok didn't know what to say, so she said, "I'll be home soon."

"I never fell asleep," So-yeon admitted.

"I'm sorry, honey. Be home soon. Go to sleep," Hyun-ok said.

"Okay," So-yeon answered.

"Okay," Hyun-ok said, hanging up. She looked over at Seogang University, took a deep breath, and headed home.

Hyun-ok arrived at the apartment. She crept through the living room and into the kitchen, where she rummaged for tofu, kimchi, and rice. She made the meal in silence, pondering on what So-yeon had said to her on the phone.

After she finished cooking the food and wrapping it in cellophane, Hyun-ok made her way into So-yeon's bedroom. Even in the dawn light, the pink in the walls gave off a warm glow. So-yeon lay on her side, eyes closed, hugging her stuffed rabbit. Hyun-ok had won that plush doll at a game stall throwing darts at balloons, and gave it to So-yeon knowing full well that she would love it.

Hyun-ok leaned in, doing her best not to disturb her daughter, and kissed her on the forehead. She said, "I know you're still not asleep."

"I love you," So-yeon said, a small smile breaking out on her face.

"I love you too," Hyun-ok said, a wan smile breaking out on her face.

Hyun-ok went into the master bedroom, to the empty bed. She shuffled into the bathroom and prepared to go to sleep. As she brushed her teeth, she saw herself in the mirror. Upon seeing her reflection, she felt the urge to sleep for ten years.

After washing her face, Hyun-ok slid into bed. She thought about the look on her daughter's face when she came home that morning, and she thought about how she used to wake up on Sunday mornings with her husband, and how they would all watch TV as a family. Now Sunday mornings consisted of her slinking around like some sort of stray cat. As Hyun-ok's limbs grew increasingly heavy, and the sensation of sleep cloaked her like a warm blanket, she thought again about So-yeon's smile. Her last conscious thought was that Seogang University didn't seem like such a bad school after all.

Orangutan

Adam refreshed the page as he took a bite of sweet, savory durian. The fruit that many called "hell on the outside, heaven on the inside" gave off a pungent aroma that was so offensive to Adam's wife that she forbade him from eating it inside the house, so he ate it out on the terrace as he checked TripAdvisor. After learning of the website earlier in the year, concerns with how guests reviewed his hostel burbled and built up in the back of his mind like water behind a new dam. The latest review, titled "Worst Guesthouse in the City of Sandakan," rated Adam's hostel at one star out of a possible five. The review had been posted two days prior:

The owner of this dump, a paunchy pig named Adam, was a negligently incompetent guide on our tour, as he drove recklessly the whole journey to the jungle and refused to stop when my girlfriend had to use the toilet. Once we were on the river cruise, the only animals we ever saw were ugly proboscis monkeys. Those dicknosed buggers are all over the place in Borneo, so nothing special there. No orangutans. No elephants.

But there were bedbugs in our room. Also there was no power, so that was great.

Adam squeezed the durian in his hands until it slid through his fingertips and dropped on the patio with a smack.

He was sure that it wasn't his fault that all of Sabah had experienced a blackout that day. This was an ongoing issue in the easternmost state of Malaysia, and Adam didn't think that it spoke to the quality of his hostel. Every other hostel in Sandakan lost power that day too, so this tourist would have been upset no matter where he stayed. As far as the animals went, Adam didn't think that seeing them was fully in his control. All he could do was try to put his customers in the best position to see them by getting them on the river around dusk, so that's what he did. Seeing orangutans had more to do with luck than it did with skill. Despite being native to northeast Borneo, he himself had never seen wild orangutans, and it certainly was not due to his incompetence, but rather their rarity.

After licking the yellow-orange fruit from his fingertips and closing TripAdvisor, he slammed the door shut as he went inside to put on his shoes. Adam never responded to negative reviews on TripAdvisor, but he imagined that if he had the chance to take this particular tourist on a jungle river cruise again, he would push him overboard and leave him for the crocodiles.

That would show him how incompetent he was. Huffing and puffing from both anger and the effort of bending over to put on his shoes, Adam grabbed the keys off the kitchen table and left the house.

If Adam's hostel, Sabah Backpackers, was going to keep up, he couldn't afford negative reviews. The vitriol was catching up to the business. Occupancy was down from previous years, and if he didn't find orangutans for guests or improve the hospitality, his problems were going to increase. That was why he had instituted the free breakfast, but apparently guests were not pleased with his thoughtfulness. The Internet was increasingly cruel to Sabah Backpackers, and Adam was struggling to reverse the tide.

Once he arrived at the hostel parking lot, Adam stopped the car and looked out at the Sulu Sea for a moment before calling the front desk. The sea was calm today, looking more like an emerald glass plate than a body of water. Adam called the front desk.

"Sabah Backpackers."

"You should be happier when you answer the phone," Adam snarled in Malay.

"I'm sorry."

"Don't be sorry, just change it."

This was received with a brief pause.

"I'm outside. Tell the guests that I'm here."

"They'll be down shortly. You should know that there's no pow—" Adam hung up before she could finish.

While waiting, Adam thought about the bedbugs, and hoped that his customers hadn't seen any. If they had, they would be in a sour mood, and it would run the risk of spoiling the entire day. If that was the case, then he might have another bad review on his hands.

When the tourists came out, he saw that they were jubilant. He wondered why they were smiling the way they were, and hoped that it was because they were happy with the hostel service. On second thought, it merely could have been because they were a young attractive couple. She was blonde, and had dimples that led Adam to believe that her smile was truly transcendent. She was dressed well for the jungle, with athletic clothing that extended to her wrists and ankles. No mosquito bites for her. The man was tall and handsome, in Adam's opinion. He was not dressed well, however, donning a neon green tank top with pink shorts. Adam figured that the young man would probably be okay, though. Having one's skin exposed ran the risk of mosquito bites and the dengue fever that sometimes came with it. Tourists didn't often get dengue fever, however. Feeling comforted by the prospect of guiding a seemingly happy couple, Adam exited the truck. Upon hearing the car door close, the tourists approached the car, and Adam waved as he walked toward them.

"I'm Adam, the owner of the hostel," he said, moving to shake the young man's hand. "I'm Sean," the young man said, limply shaking Adam's outstretched hand. "This is Allie."

"Hi," the young woman said, beaming at Adam.

"Are you ready to go to the jungle?" Adam asked.

The couple laughed and said that they were.

"We're stoked," Sean said.

As they entered the running truck and buckled in, Adam informed them that they were aiming to arrive in the jungle just in time for dusk, when the majority of the animals came to the banks to drink.

As they pulled out of the parking lot, Allie cleared her throat. "Can I just say something?" she said. "There was no power in the hostel this morning."

"Really?" Adam said. "My employees hadn't told me." He glanced at Allie in the rearview mirror and noticed her green eyes. "There have been blackouts in Sandakan, and the rest of Sabah actually, for the past couple weeks." He attempted to look at Sean, but the angle of the mirror wouldn't allow it.

"Why do they keep happening?" Sean asked.

Adam looked in the rearview mirror and allowed his eyes to linger on Allie's. "Nobody knows. All of us in Sabah are really mad at the government, because it's not a problem in the rest of Malaysia. We're pissed off," he said, forcing a smile. A car pulled out in front of the truck.

Adam brought his eyes back to the road and slammed on the breaks just before he hit a car. He honked.

Sean and Allie lurched forward.

"Sorry," Adam said with a chuckle. "People don't know how to drive." Allie giggled, but Adam knew it was a fake laugh.

"We should have stayed in Kuala Lumpur," Sean muttered. Adam wasn't meant to hear it, but he did.

"But then we wouldn't be able to see orangutans," Allie whispered.

"We probably won't see them anyway," Sean grumbled.

Adam thought about telling the couple that seeing orangutans was all but guaranteed, but that would betray the fact that he'd been eavesdropping. Instead he noticed the ring on Sean's finger and said, "I like your ring."

Sean twisted the cobalt ring on his finger and said, "This? Thank you. She got it for me in Kota Kinabalu."

"I told you it was nice," Allie said.

"You have good taste," Adam said.

"If we hadn't come out here, we would have never visited Kota Kinabalu, and you never would've gotten that ring."

"That's true. And KK is a pretty nice city, I guess."

Allie looked away from Sean and said, "I really liked the Wet Market there."

Adam perked up as if she had brought out a durian. "That's a great place," he said. "Did you get the tuna steak?"

"I didn't see that!" Allie said. "This guy made me leave early because he wanted to find a club."

"No real clubs in KK," Adam said. He knew that there were clubs in Kuala Lumpur, but didn't want to anger Sean.

"That's what I said, but Sean doesn't listen."

Sean shrugged his shoulders and said, "I try."

"This is our first trip together," Allie added, grabbing Sean's hand.

Adam slouched in his seat. "That's great," he said. "Is it your honeymoon?"

"No," Sean said with a laugh. "We've only just started dating."

"No commitments," Allie said.

Sean scoffed. "You're in love with me."

"I doubt that very much," Allie said.

Adam laughed.

They had been on the road for an hour when they entered what was very clearly a palm plantation. The trees were lined up in perfect rows, creating what looked like a synthetic jungle. Palm oil was one of Malaysia's biggest exports, and this was how many people in Sabah made a living. Most tourists rode through the plantation without commenting on how this was the reason orangutans were going extinct, but the ones who did were often angered by them. This was the part of the drive where Adam typically tried to keep his guests distracted.

He said, "How long do you plan on staying in Malaysia?"

Sean cleared his throat and replied, "How many orangutans do you think we'll see today?"

Adam coughed and said, "I've seen them a bunch of times. I'm pretty lucky, though. Most people have never seen them." He added, "Maybe we'll get lucky today. If we do, will you give me a good review on TripAdvisor?"

"I know they're endangered, but why are they so hard to find?" Sean asked. It was clear that his attention was on orangutans, but Allie's gaze was fixed on the fields.

"There aren't many of them. They might be extinct fifteen years from now," Adam replied. "And they're shy. They avoid people." He winced, hoping that this comment didn't veer too closely to the subject of palm plantations. "Did you know, Allie, that 'orang' means 'person,' and 'hutan' means 'forest'? So 'orangutan' means 'Person of the forest'?"

"Yeah, I looked it up online," Allie said, her eyes still out the window.

Before Adam could say anything else, Sean joined Allie in looking out at the endless rows of palm.

"We'll see a lot of other animals today, too," Adam continued. "Proboscis monkeys, macaques, crocodiles, birds. Maybe elephants, if we're lucky. Proboscis monkeys—"

"All of those animals would be cool," she interrupted. "But orangutans would be best." Her attention was away from the expanse of palms, at least. Sean's attention, however, was not on orangutans anymore, but the fields. Adam lamented that he couldn't keep both of them focused at the same time.

He tried the proboscis monkey angle again. "Did you know that when proboscis monkeys were first discovered, people didn't think they were actually monkeys? Because of their long nose."

"I really hate that I have to see this, you know," Sean said, gesturing out the window. "What do you mean?" Adam asked, feigning ignorance while looking into the rearview mirror at his guest.

"All of these palm trees lined up like crops. This is why the orangutans are hard to find. People cut down their homes to make room for the palm trees, and then they've got nothing."

"It's a really difficult situation for us," said Adam.

"I don't think it's difficult. If you stop creating palm plantations, you stop killing orangutans. Simple to me." He smirked and gave Allie a sideways glance.

"There are a lot of efforts to protect orangutans, you know. The Sepilok Orangutan Sanctuary is a good example. They rescue orphaned orangutans and work with them until they are ready to be released back into the wild." Adam knew he had to sound diplomatic if he wanted a good review.

"The world is so greedy," Sean said. He pulled an energy bar out of his pocket and opened it. "I'll only be happy today if we see orangutans."

"We'll see them; you don't need to worry about that," Adam said. He was worried.

"It would really be a let down if we didn't see any," Allie said. She moved her eyes from the palm plantation to Adam's eyes in the mirror. "I'd hate to come all the way out here only to be disappointed."

Adam squirmed and caught a glimpse of the bar in Sean's hand. He asked, "What flavor is that?" He knew, but wanted Sean to say it out loud.

"Peanut butter. It's my favorite," Sean said, taking a bite.

Adam was aware that peanut butter contained palm oil, but didn't say anything. "Looks good." He tallied the small victory internally.

"It is good."

"Maybe Allie is a good luck charm!" Adam said, stealing another glance at Allie. "Elephants are the rarest animals out there," he added. "The only time I saw them was when I brought my daughter out. She was the good luck charm."

"Well that's cool," Sean said.

"Now that I think of it — you kind of remind me of her," Adam said, as his reflected gaze settled on her. "She has dimples, too."

"Really? That's nice of you to say," she said.

"If your daughter looks anything like Allie, then she must be hot," Sean said.

"My daughter's fourteen," Adam replied, keeping both hands on the wheel.

Sean tried to walk his comment back, but it didn't amount to much. Allie glared at him.

Adam turned on the radio, and "Havoc" by Joe Flizzow pulsed out of the speakers.

The couple cringed to the Malay music for the next fifteen minutes. Adam smiled in the rearview and asked, "Do you like this?"

Allie said, "It's different."

Sean said, "It's not my cup of tea."

Before Adam could ask Sean why, Allie said, "Your taste in music is garbage anyway." Adam stifled a laugh.

"What do you mean?" Sean said.

"All you listen to is Pitbull. Enough's enough."

"You don't like Pitbull?" Adam chimed in.

"Sorry I like positive music," Sean said.

"Try listening to 'Elephant Gun' by Beirut. It might have more positive energy than any song I've ever heard," Allie said.

"Whatever you say," Sean replied.

"I'll play it for you when we get back to the hostel tonight."

"If there's power."

Adam tightened his grip on the steering wheel and drove faster.

About an hour out from the departure point for their jungle river cruise, Adam took his guests to a small restaurant just off the highway. No walls separated the place from the surrounding jungle, which allowed the symphony of its residents' calls to wash over the diners along with the tropical breeze. Adam ordered the tom yum soup and a Tiger beer. The cooks had gone a little heavy on the lemongrass. Adam hoped that they hadn't seasoned his guests' plates as liberally. Allie ordered the same thing and seemed to be impressed, which relaxed Adam.

Sean ordered nasi lemak with beef rendang and a Carlsberg. He mused that he couldn't visit a country like Malaysia without trying its national dish. The coconut cream rice came out wrapped in a banana leaf with the tender beef on the side. The sight of the plate made Adam consider sending back the tom yum soup and ordering it for himself, but when Sean tried it, he complained that it tasted too much like coconut. Adam clenched his jaw.

"So where are you two from?" He asked.

"California, and she's from Chicago," Sean said.

"They don't eat coconut in California," Allie said.

"Sorry I didn't like *nasi lemak*," Sean replied, drawing out the name of the dish. "In my hometown — San Clemente — every restaurant has seafood caught fresh that would blow this place out of the water."

Before Adam could suppress his true feelings and ask whether or not Sean was a surfer, Allie cut in and said, "Nobody cares about San Clemente. We're out here in this beautiful jungle, and you just want to brag about your hometown?"

"Well, he asked," he protested.

"Do you still wear your letter jacket? Just shut up and enjoy the experience we're having."

Adam had never been attracted to American blondes before, but this statement changed his mind about that. He didn't know what a letter jacket was, but he liked the sound of the insult. It was the first time he'd ever seen someone dress a white guy down in this way, and he was thoroughly impressed.

She turned to Adam and added, "I think we're going to find orangutans today." For the first time, he was certain that they would.

After settling the bill, the group hit the road again to delve deeper into the jungle. There were no palm plantations on the rest of the drive, which Adam observed with a sense of relief.

As he'd done after the palm oil rant, he drove about as fast as he could, zipping past the occasional motorist at about 150 km/h. He made it his mission to get to the river as soon as possible.

With about two hours to spare before dusk, the pickup truck rolled into the point in the jungle that they would embark from. It was a hamlet on the banks of the Kinabatangan River, and Adam assumed that it was unlike anything the American couple had ever seen. Corrugated tin huts peeked out from behind flaky orange Pelawan trees like toddlers playing hide-and-seek. Not an inch of the village was paved; the tamped brown earth served as the town's artery to civilization.

Children played in the road, and Adam lightly tapped on the horn to get them to disperse. The splayed palms and white-barked Mengaris trees provided a canopy over the village so that most of it was living in perpetual shade. The car bumped and rolled to a slow stop in a clearing that, for anyone who had not visited as much as Adam, would have been impossible to find. A shack and a small wooden outboard boat awaited them on the bank of the muddy river. The white paint on its hull was chipped away, revealing the red cedar underneath. Standing next to the shack was Adam's boatman and sole contact in this remote forest, a beanpole of a man named Fariz. As he shut off the ignition in the truck, Adam turned to his guests and said, "Welcome to the jungle."

While Sean and Allie took selfies with the jungle scenery as their background, Adam approached Fariz, shook his hand, and said, "Selamat tengah hari."

Fariz greeted him back.

Adam continued in Malay, saying, "Have you scouted for orangutans today?" Fariz shook his head.

"I told you to do that. You know I'm relying on orang-utans to keep my hostel open."

"And I told you that I can't. The boat needs gas, and I don't want to drive into Sandakan any more than I have to to get it."

"If I keep getting negative reviews, you won't have money to get any gas."

"Don't worry. Orangutans are getting easier to see."

Adam scoffed. "What do you mean by that? More of them are dying."

Fariz laughed. "All of the other tour guides know the reason, but you don't. You'll see today."

Adam squinted his eyes and cocked his head sideways in the way a puppy does when it hears a high-pitched sound. Before Adam could articulate a response, Sean approached and asked, "Is everything alright?"

Adam put on a fake smile and said, in English, "Yes, everything's fine. Fariz here just told me a good joke."

Sean giggled. "What was it?"

Adam's smile disappeared. "What?"

"What did Fariz say?"

Adam stalled for a moment before saying, "It doesn't translate to English well. Are we ready to go?"

"I'll grab Allie," Sean said as he walked over to his girlfriend.

Adam turned to Fariz and shrugged his shoulders.

"You'll see," Fariz said.

Everyone put on tattered life vests. The vests, which had been a vibrant orange in the past, were worn from the sun. The smell of them, which used to be that of new shoes, was dank and musty from the rain. Fariz hopped onboard first and pulled the starter cord. The engine, like a lazy dog unwilling to forfeit its place on the kitchen floor, puttered and protested. It was only after three hearty pulls and a bead of sweat off his brow that Fariz was able to get the motor running, and it was then that

Adam joined him onboard. The boat rocked gently from side to side. The muddy water rippled outward from its undercarriage. Sean and Allie joined the men on the boat and sat close to the front so that they could get a clear view. Sean whispered to Allie that the stiff bench was already making his tailbone sore, but Allie ignored him. Adam checked that his guests were comfortable and ready to go, and sat next to Fariz at the stern. They sat there to operate the motor and counteract the weight of the tourists in the front. Once everyone was seated, Fariz directed the boat downstream. The vessel wedged through the water like a dull knife through cold butter as the crew embarked on their mission to encounter wildlife.

The river opened up wide in front of them. The jungle respired all around them, its trees shaking and waving as it drew the travelers into its deep, dark underbelly. The couple gazed in wonderment as they passed dense thickets, as well as roots exposed on sheer cliff faces squirming and squiggling all the way down to the brown river to get a taste of the gritty broth. With better access to the river, mangroves menacingly crept in toward the boat, their snarled tendrils seeking to ensnare the visitors.

The first animal to appear was a hornbill. Similar to a toucan but larger and with a pale bill, it flew across the river in the distance. Adam pointed it out to Allie so that she could take a picture. The bird perched on a branch and glanced at the boat behind its hooked beak before taking off.

"Was that a toucan?" Sean asked Adam, turning around so that he could be heard over the motor. "Like Toucan Sam?"

"What?"

"You know, the bird on the Froot Loops box," he added.

"I don't know what you're talking about. That was a hornbill."

"You don't know anything," Sean muttered.

Adam pretended that he hadn't heard Sean over the motor.

They came upon a colony of proboscis monkeys, so Fariz drew the boat to a stop. The monkeys' most striking feature was their pendulous noses, which were long, floppy appendages dangling over their mouths. These monkeys were unlike any other primate in the world, but sharing the trees with the orangutans meant that in terms of fame, these creatures were overshadowed. That, and most people considered them ugly.

"They look so weird," Sean said, focusing his phone on the orange monkeys.

When they were parked in front of the troop, Adam leaned in close to Allie's ear and told her, "Proboscis monkeys. We call them Dutchmen."

She kept her eyes on the animals and asked, "Why do you call them Dutchmen?"

"Because Dutchmen are dick faces!" He laughed, but she only gave him a hesitant chuckle. Adam's stomach dropped and his face grew hot. His joke hadn't landed in the way he thought it would. He chided himself for assuming that Allie would laugh at it.

Unfazed by Adam's laughter, the gang of monkeys stared at the boat in unison, their beady eyes dead set on Allie. Away from the bank, some of the monkeys leapt from branch to branch. Leaves rustled in a frenzy. The boat rode its natural momentum and idled past the troop. Fariz pulled the starter cord, the motor caught on the first try, and they got going. The proboscis monkeys continued to stare at the boat as it pressed on.

No matter how many times he saw them, Adam was always dumbfounded by these oddities of Borneo. More than any animal outside of perhaps the orangutan, the Proboscis monkey was the most wary of humans; it was almost as if that characteristic appendage granted them a keen perception unattainable for other primates.

After the group spotted out more animals — specifically cranes, silver macaques, cattle, crocodiles, and more hornbills and Proboscis monkeys — the sun drew lower.

This was the furthest along the river that Adam had gone in awhile. As the boat pressed on, he looked out in surprise. Ahead of the boat, the sky grew much bigger as the Mengaris and Pelawan disappeared. The group had come to the end of the jungle. In its place were more palm plantations, and Adam looked at Fariz. Fariz nodded.

Sean said, "What do you know, more palm trees."

Adam said, "I guess it's time to go back."

"Keep your eyes on the trees," Fariz said as he turned the boat around.

"Are we not going to see any orangutans?" Sean asked.

"It doesn't look that way," Adam said. "But let's see. We might see them on the way back to the hamlet."

"But that's the whole reason we came all the way out here."

"It's never a guarantee that we will see anything. There is a much greater chance of seeing orangutans at the sanctuary, but that's different from seeing them in the true wild."

"The only way that I'll even think of giving you a good TripAdvisor review is if we see orangutans," Sean said.

"Don't worry," Adam said, although he was himself.

Allie let her finger scrape the surface of the water, creating a new ripple. "We're lucky to be able to come out here and see all of these animals."

"I completely agree," Adam said.

"What we saw is not enough for me," Sean said.

Adam kept his eyes in the trees the whole way upriver, hoping they would get lucky.

They were going to be reaching the dock soon, and their opportunity to see wild orangutans was dwindling with every second. Adam sighed, resigned to the fact that he would most likely never see one in the wild.

Just then, Fariz whispered, "Look up at the tree. Orangutan."

Adam's chest contracted and his eyes darted from branch to branch before he finally saw it, a reddish brown ball at the top of a tree three meters from the bank. It was a male, with the characteristic flanges extending from each side of his face. The orangutan gazed out at them, and Adam knew when he looked into its eyes that he was looking at another soul. He was staring directly at a complex person. He thought that if he were to shout out, "Selamat tengah hari," it would nod and wave. He felt as if he were in a dream, vividly seeing something that was unreasonable in a realistic sense but made perfect sense in this context. All of Adam's worries about his hostel and the TripAdvisor reviews dissolved in the gaze of the orangutan. His focus on the orangutan was so intense that a halo of light seemed to form around the ape. He didn't care about anything else in that moment, not even the power outages at his hostel. The Person of the Forest had a belly as prodigious as Adam's and was even snacking on a durian. This amused Adam and made him question why people had such an insatiable taste for palm oil. He reached to tap Sean on the shoulder, because he knew that this was the only chance they would have to see an orangutan. Just before his fingers made contact with Sean's sunburned shoulder, however, he drew it back. He brought his gaze back to the orangutan in the tree and smiled. Fariz patted his shoulder before the orangutan swung further into the forest.

"Why did we stop?" Sean asked.

"They were looking in the trees but haven't found anything," Allie replied.

"That's exactly right," Adam said.

Fariz restarted the boat.

Adam said, "Look. More Proboscis monkeys."

It was in fact the same troop they had seen earlier. The monkeys, as if in a show of mockery, started up a hooting chorus. They took on the appearance of a gallery of old men, all shouting at the tourists to go bother someone else. Adam laughed and patted Fariz on the shoulder. Fariz joined Adam and the monkeys in laughter.

"What's so funny?" Sean asked.

Adam took a moment to catch his breath. Then he said, "It's all of the Dutchmen I see. Every day."

Fariz laughed as Sean and Allie looked at each other. He sped the boat up and took everyone back to the docking point.

As everyone took off their life vests, Sean said, "This was the worst idea. I still wish we would have stayed in Kuala Lumpur."

"I'm sorry, Sean," Allie said. "You can pick what we do with our next vacation." She slipped off her vest, tossed it on the ground, and walked to the truck.

Sean directed his attention to Adam and said, "I thought you saw orangutans every time you came out here."

Through a smile, Adam said, "We must have been really unlucky this time. I don't know what it was."

Sean shook his head and walked back to the truck. Adam bid Fariz farewell and followed.

The following morning, as Adam ate durian on his veranda, he cast his eyes out to the Sulu Sea. The thought of checking Trip Advisor to see how bad Sean's review of Sabah Backpackers had been didn't even cross his mind. All he could think about as he looked out at the calm sea was the male orangutan in the tree, durian in hand, begging him to keep people away from his home.

Grand Opening

In terms of importance, Fai saw today as greater than the day of her wedding, the days her second and third children were born, and comparable to the day her first son was born. Today was the day that she would finally accomplish her lifelong dream of opening up a restaurant in Tsim Sha Tsui. The location was even better than she'd envisioned, as it was perfectly equidistant from the Star Ferry dock and the Avenue of Stars. She could look one direction and see the two-deck, green-and-white remnant of the Victorian age chugging into port, and look the other direction and practically see the Bruce Lee statue, perpetually standing balanced and flexed in anticipation of a fight. Apart from these landmarks, Tsim Sha Tsui was the major shopping district of the city. Whether it was for designer clothes or a knockoff bag, there was no shortage of options. Even Jenny Bakery, home to butter cookies so appetizing that tourists bought and promptly stuffed tins of them into their luggage, was located in Tsim Sha Tsui. Knockoff bakeries, attempting to imitate Jenny's tin in order to dupe naive tourists into buying their inferior product, were located in Tsim Sha Tsui as well. One of them was called "Jinny Bakery." In short, Fai's newest restaurant was where everything in Hong Kong was happening.

She had opened up her first restaurant ten years prior, and while it was a huge success, it wasn't close enough to the bustle of Tsim Sha Tsui for her to be satisfied. Her two teenage sons would be heading off to university soon, and she had dreams of sending them abroad for that. In addition to her boys, one careless night after signing the lease led to a baby daughter who would require the plushest possible upbringing. No public school for her. International only. The neighborhood was prime real estate, and despite the astronomical rent, Fai was attracted there like a raccoon to trash as soon as a lot became available and she had the means to afford it. The only problem with the lease, and the biggest distraction for Fai on the day of her restaurant's opening, was the fact that the building the restaurant was in was owned by Sun Hung Kai Properties. The Kwok brothers, who were co-chairmen of the development corporation, were set to go on trial in a few days' time for taking massive bribes.

All of Fai's relatives were in attendance for the grand opening, even those from the Mainland. The men wore freshly pressed suits while each woman wore a cheongsam. Fai made sure that her dress was the most beautiful of all, as it was a white number with embroidered lotuses dominating the design and putting all of the others to shame.

Everyone had a particular role in this event because they knew that if they had not offered to contribute, they would draw the type of ire for which she was notorious. She was not a woman one wanted to cross. In her mid-forties, and with a brow perpetually furrowed, she'd gotten her start as a vendor at the famous Temple Street Market. It was there that the lines for her beef chow fun and egg tarts clogged the thoroughfare. In addition to serving up cuisine so delectable that Anthony Bourdain once featured her on one of his shows, she made the type of friends who could elevate her career, eventually meeting the Kwok brothers. They said they loved her beef chow fun, and that was the first step to her gaining entry into Tsim Sha Tsui.

Those closest to her had the most crucial roles to play in today's festivities. Her sister had been in charge of making a lion, so she commissioned all of her friends from the market to do so, and the responsibility of Fai's two sons for the day was to carry out the lion dance. Her husband Koeng had hired a photographer just for the occasion, and a traditional band stood off to the side, ready to start playing once the red and white confetti rained down from the second-story balcony.

Fai called to Koeng as everyone slowly congregated in front of the restaurant.

"Yes?"

"Where's the photographer?"

"He's right there," Koeng said, pointing at the bald man fiddling with a camera.

"Okay. Everything has to go right today," Koeng patted her shoulder and said, "I know."

Fai removed his hand and said, "No you don't. If the Kwoks get convicted, who knows what will happen to this building? There will probably be new owners. And the only way the new owners will keep us here is if everyone knows we're the best. Like the way Din Tai Fung is in Taipei."

"Those dumplings are all over the world now."

"We need to be that good to stay in this building." Fai looked over her shoulder at the blue glass tower.

Koeng took a deep breath and said, "Sun Hung Kai is a huge company. Nothing's going to happen if the Kwoks are guilty."

"You don't know that," Fai asserted. She scanned the crowd to make sure everything was in place. Then she turned to Koeng and said, "You told Jasmine not to come, right? It won't look good for me if my maid comes to my opening."

Koeng looked at his shoes and said, "Yes, I told her."

"Good," Fai said as she smiled for the camera. Through her teeth she said, "She doesn't know how to fold laundry the right way, so she will definitely mess something up today."

Fai had specifically planned for the grand opening of her restaurant to take place on a Monday, because Monday wasn't Sunday. All of the maids in Hong Kong were required by law to leave the houses they worked in on Sundays, and Fai knew that a maid out of the house was a maid more likely to stop by her restaurant.

As thunder rumbled behind the clouds, the photographer went through the group and made adjustments for the picture. He turned shoulders, straightened collars, and dusted off shoulders. The photo was to be framed, displayed in the family's living room, and dusted by Jasmine, so Fai wanted it to be perfect. Fai of course was front and center with Koeng at her side, and their sons peeked out from under the bamboo papered lion in order to be visible for the portrait. The photographer beckoned for everyone's attention and prepared to snap a photograph.

Just before the photographer took the picture, however, Fai noticed a group of foreigners standing on the other side of the street. It was a group of five young people — a tall white man in a green shirt held hands with a blonde woman in a blue summer dress. A shorter woman with curly black hair and what looked to be three gold bracelets on each wrist watched the scene in front of the restaurant, and two other men in cutoff t-shirts stood next to her. They were a little bit too close to each other for Fai's liking. Fai thought she saw their hands brush together, and it made her shiver.

The photographer took the picture before Fai was able to bring her focus back to the lens, so the first photograph was no good. Fai told the photographer to snap another one. She didn't care how many pictures they had to take — as long as they were done before the rain and she looked good in the final portrait, she would be satisfied.

Once the barrage of photographs was complete, the confetti fell from the balcony, the band played their music, and her sons started their lion dance. They hopped and gamboled about to the festive din, and everyone in the immediate area grinned and clapped. Fai observed her sons with a watchful eye, internally noting that their performance was not nearly as good as that of the professionals. She momentarily thought that she should have hired a troupe before she saw everyone's jovial expressions. They hadn't noticed the series of missteps her second son had made, but she had. She'd have a word with him later, when scolding him wouldn't serve to embarrass her in front of others.

She stole a glance at the other side of the street and noticed that the group of foreigners was no longer there. She wondered whether they had left as she hugged and shook hands with those in attendance, and once the music concluded, everyone on the front steps of the restaurant tramped over the red and white confetti and into the newly minted establishment. The rain followed.

Red carpet and gold linings were the theme of the new restaurant, as Fai wanted to keep the decor consistent with that of her first establishment. Unlike that first restaurant, however, the carpet did not yet smell of musty hoisin sauce and coriander. The very same laminated menu Fai had used at her Temple Street Market stall hung on the wall behind the podium that harbored the register. This was another clue that she wanted to keep the same level of quality that had made her stall famous in the first place. Upward mobility was a beautiful thing in Hong Kong, but the type that she enjoyed was so rare that it could never be given away.

The aspect of running a restaurant that annoyed Fai most was delegating as opposed to cooking all of the cuisine herself. Given the opportunity to be frank, most of her employees both prior and current would characterize her as a micromanager. Some might use less savory terms. Even with this in mind, all of Fai's best employees followed her to the new Tsim Sha Tsui location because they knew that while she was sometimes a pain to work for, she was going to succeed in her newest venture. When she did succeed, she would be surprisingly generous with her rewards. At the first location, when sales far exceeded all projections, she granted everyone on the payroll a bonus of three months' salary for the Lunar New Year. That bonus was the only reason anyone tolerated her management style.

In the kitchen, the staff was ready for the first wave of customers. They had to get their bearings at the beginning of the day, as the locations of the pots, pans, utensils, and everything else were different from what they were used to. For this, as well as basic food preparation, Fai made everyone come in hours before opening. By the time the doors opened, all of the necessary adjustments had been made. Herbs were chopped, vegetables were julienned, and sauces were mixed. When she came into the kitchen to inspect the work that her staff had done, Fai sampled everything in front of her, circling her jaw like a sommelier might swirl a glass of pinot noir. The staff held their towels in both hands and stared at the ground as their boss scrutinized their work, and when she approved of everything prepared, they let out a collective sigh of relief and commenced the real work.

The first wave of the day comprised primarily family and friends, of course, although the group of foreigners had managed

to enter as well. This excited Fai. She'd served high-profile customers before, but it never changed the fact that she loved
serving people from other countries. Anthony Bourdain was
the best person she could have possibly served, because he was
both famous *and* foreign. In the present moment, Fai felt that
she needed to impress the foreigners most of all, because her
family and friends were already familiar with her reputation.
They would not be surprised by the quality of what she was
serving. These people, however, did not know anything about
her and most likely did not know anything about Cantonese
cuisine in general, so she knew that she had a rare opportunity.
She wanted to serve them a dish so delectable that they would
go back to America, Britain, or wherever they were from and
brag to all of their friends about the real Chinese food that
they'd had in Hong Kong. It would ruin American Chinese food
for them forever, which she considered to be a good thing. No
person in their right mind needed to eat that sad excuse for food.
That style of food didn't even discriminate between the Eight
Great Regional Cuisines! Fai didn't know what General Tso's
chicken tasted like, and she didn't want to find out. She thought
the idea of American Chinese food was so gross and insulting
that she equated it to fish food. With this in mind, she was up
to the self-imposed challenge of blowing these tourists away.

Sitting at the gold-rimmed rectangular table in the middle
of the room and looking at the laminated, ring-bound menu
in front of them, the group clearly had no idea what they were
looking at. The good news for them was that Fai had the fore-
sight to include pictures of dishes in the menus, which was a
feature that the menus of her first restaurant did not have. This
location, being in such a tourist-heavy area, necessitated such a
detail. There was nothing more annoying to her than a group
of Westerners not knowing what they were ordering, only to

assertively point at an item on the menu and later take exception to the food that they received. Fai felt that the tendency was rooted in the assumption that all Hong Kongers knew English due to the city's previous status as a British colony, but the fact was that Cantonese predominated, with Mandarin growing increasingly pervasive since the handover. Fai had seen the cluelessness routine play out numerous times at her first location, and by now assumed that complaining about meals and insulting wait staff was an American custom.

The current group of tourists pored over the laminated booklets, their eyes scrunching up as they looked at the items on the menu. The two men who Fai thought were gay pointed and laughed at one of the items, and the curly-headed girl joined them. The young man in the green shirt looked at them as if he wanted to join in the laughter, but the blonde gave him a look that caused his eyes to shoot back down at the menu. The group wasn't ready to order, so Fai let them be. She checked on all of the other tables and found that everyone was enjoying themselves.

Each person immediately said that their food was terrific when asked. Fai saw her second son standing idly at the other side of the room and motioned him over.

"What are you doing?" she hissed.

"Watching the room, Mom."

"Go fold some napkins," Fai said while looking at the table of foreigners.

"We have napkins already."

Fai glared at her son. "Is this your restaurant?"

Her son took the hint and went into the kitchen.

Fai crossed her arms and looked over at the foreigners' table. The blonde woman in the sundress made eye contact with her and motioned her over.

Normally Fai would send a server over to take the order and later reprimand them for any mistake they had made, but the challenge of impressing this group compelled her to take the order herself.

The order consisted of three servings of beef chow fun for the men, with Fai assuming they wanted it because the men had seen plates of stir-fried beef on most of the other tables; tea-smoked duck for the blonde, which Fai admired because it was more intrepid; and choy sum for the woman with curly black hair, who gestured and pointed that she did not want shrimp with her stir-fried vegetables. Fai assumed that this woman was a vegetarian, and thought her weaker for it. She liked the blonde woman more because of her ability to take control. As soon as the orders were complete, Fai took the menus, smiled at the blonde, and walked to the kitchen.

The kitchen was hotter than the dining area by about ten degrees, and condensed water dribbled down the white tile walls. Cooks barked orders at each other over the hissing woks, but fell silent as soon as their eyes caught Fai. She positioned herself in front of the cooks. She scanned the line and let her eyes settle on the newest cook — a thin man with glistening forearms.

"Don't just look at me," she said "There are still people out there waiting for food."

"Yes ma'am," the new cook said with a nervous swallow. He stood fiddling with his fingers.

"You aren't cooking yet. Are you trying to insult my family by withholding food from them?"

"No ma'am," he said as he started to vigorously stir fry the vegetables he'd previously been working on.

She grabbed an apron from the steel shelf behind her, tied it on over her cheongsam, and said, "Slower. Have you ever cooked vegetables before?"

He stopped cooking and stuttered.

Before he could spit out his response, she said, "'Slower' does not mean stop."

He started again and said, "I'm sorry, ma'am. I just wanted to show you that I was working hard."

"If you cared about your job, you would know that you should stir fry vegetables at a consistent rate, not at the stop-and-go pace that you seem to think is effective. Get out of my kitchen."

"I'm sorry?"

"Apparently you don't have ears now, either. Bo," she said, pointing to the cook on the left of the disgraced employee. "Take over for this peasant."

The young man knew that he would not be paid for the day, and while that was deflating, he also knew that any sort of protest would lead to him no longer having a job, so he simply took his apron off and walked out, careful to display the correct level of disappointment. Too much would lead to Fai accusing him of being sycophantic, whereas too little would lead to her accusing him of apathy. Fai stepped into his place before he was out the back door. She started by sliding the suspended receipts, denoting the disgraced one's orders, in front of Bo. She then prepared the ingredients for the order that she had just taken. There was a zero percent chance of her entrusting the foreigners' order to her cooks, especially after the display that she had just witnessed.

When she started cooking the five meals, she did so with an alacrity that reminded everyone of why she had been able to rise to her current position in the first place. Every motion she made, whether it was a chop, scoop, or a pour, was completed with diamond-cutting precision. Upon seeing Koeng stroll through the kitchen and grab a ready-made bowl of Lanzhou beef lamian, she ordered him to keep an eye on the table of tourists, because she knew that they would expect someone to dote on them and tell them what to do with the sauces on their table.

She also told him to notify them that their meals would be out shortly, ignoring the fact that he was worse at English than she was. He gave her a firm nod as he swung the door open with his elbow.

When Fai brought all of the meals out on a single tray, she saw something peculiar. The female foreigners were bickering at each other, with the male one in a green shirt attempting to defuse the situation. The first concern to come to Fai's mind was whether the conflict had disturbed anyone else's experience in the restaurant. It evidently hadn't, as everyone was still focused on their own meals and conversations, so she breathed a sigh of relief. She approached the table and was greeted with a palpable silence as she set down the dishes in front of her elbow-scratching patrons. Before she was able to tell them to enjoy their meal in English, the blonde one restarted the argument with the noirette one. While Fai was far from fluent, she was certain that she heard the phrases, "you like my boyfriend," and, "I can't trust you," thrown around. The green-shirted man, who seemed to be the blonde's boyfriend, tried to calm her by putting his hands on her shoulder, but it was no use. She stood up and stormed out of the restaurant, ignoring the rain. She hadn't touched her tea-smoked duck. The sleeveless men, who had remained silent throughout the spat, followed her out in solidarity. When it had all settled, the boyfriend in the green shirt, the black-haired woman with the bracelets, and five steaming meals remained.

The steam rising from the duck slowed its pace, and eventually it stopped emanating as the duck's brown skin tightened and its bumps grew more visible. The beef in the chow fun servings grew gray from cooking on the plate as the pair of foreigners ate their meals in silence. Fai looked at the leftover food and a sharp sense of disgust grew in her throat. She hated waste, but wasn't going to give any of the abandoned food to her staff, either, because that would give them a pretense for taking a break. She could not afford this, and it might even lead to the staff making bigger portions in the future with the idea of eating whatever remained. She was not pleased, and as long as there was a conflict taking place in her restaurant, she wanted to correct the situation.

She approached the young man, jabbed him on his arm, and did her best to ask what the problem was.

He recoiled from her touch and looked at her curiously.

She repeated herself, anunciating her pidgin English so that he would understand it. He replied with a sentence that contained the words, "jealous," and, "not understand."

Figuring that the conflict was an issue of communication, as is usually the case in romantic relationships, she attempted to get the boyfriend to go outside by pulling the green cloth on his shoulder upward, pointing out the door, and saying, "Go. Talk."

The curly-haired woman shook her head and waved her arms. Her bracelets jingled as she said, "Too mad."

Fai saw a gleam in the female tourist's eyes that told her that she was not as weak as she'd suspected. It seemed, however, that this young woman was caught in an uncomfortable position. Fai guessed that this girl had done enough for the girl in the dress to think that she was trying to steal her boyfriend. Fai pointed down at the boyfriend and tried to ask the noirette if she liked him.

The young woman understood Fai's English much better than the others had, and the restaurateur respected her for it.

As soon as Fai had finished asking about her desires, the young woman nodded, and her eyes welled up. The man in the green shirt dropped his chin to his chest and scratched the back of his head.

Fai didn't like that this pair was being awkward together. So what if the woman in the sundress was angry? If the curly-headed woman liked this young man, she should do what she can to make the relationship happen. Fai wished she could tell her about the value of assertiveness and how it got her this restaurant, and cursed herself for not being better at English. All she could do was point at the young man, give a thumbs up, and leave this "new couple" alone together. After she left, she continued to sneak glances at them as often as she could.

The duo dined quickly and conversed surreptitiously, careful not to do or say anything that the woman in the sundress could interpret as adulterous if she were to walk back into the restaurant. The most scandalous moment, however, was near the end of the meal, when the boyfriend attempted to reach over the table to touch his counterpart's shoulder. When he tried this, she recoiled. Fai read this resistance as coquettish in a way, and fancied the young woman to be telling her date that she had strong, irrepressible feelings for him, but that the timing of it all just wasn't right. Fai imagined that the young woman was saying that if he were to break up with the other woman diplomatically, so as to not make her seem like a home-wrecker, they could be together at last. Fai thoroughly enjoyed this exercise of putting words in the duo's mouths, and it made her feel like she was watching a Korean drama.

This fantastical drama was soon replaced by a much more immediate type of drama for Fai, as Jasmine strolled into the restaurant. She held the baby at her side. Fai grew irate the moment the bells on the door clinked and signaled her entrance. To her, Jasmine's presence was a personal affront; an attempt to defile the day's festivities by exposing everyone to her loathsome presence. On a day that meant this much to Fai, there was no room for what she considered to be the less savory aspects of her life.

"Hello, Mrs. Lam," Jasmine said in broken Cantonese. "Your daughter and I wanted to visit you and try your food."

Fai stared coldly at the woman who changed her baby's diapers on a daily basis. Jasmine bounced the baby up, adjusting her grip. "Can we eat?"

"Didn't I tell you to stay at the apartment and watch the baby? She doesn't like crowds."

"Yes, ma'am, but I think she wanted to see you."

Fai crossed her arms, and nearly all of the patrons in the restaurant turned to observe the confrontation. Even the foreign couple looked in Jasmine's direction. Fai said, "It seems to me that you are the one who wanted to see me. Clearly you knew that I would be in good spirits on the day that I opened up my crown jewel of a restaurant, and you thought that you could exploit my enthusiasm and get a free meal out of it. You even had the nerve to bring my daughter as a way to play on my weaknesses as a mother. But you don't know me like you think you know me. And I am well aware of the type of woman you are, Jasmine, and I see through every disingenuous gesture."

Jasmine struggled to come up with a response, and the baby fussed in her arms. "I'm confused. We just want to see you on your big day, I promise." She bounced the baby in an effort to calm her.

"Do you know one of the more difficult aspects of owning a dog?"

"A dog?"

"Yes, a dog. The problem with owning one as a pet is that they always try to tell their owner that they love them. Their persistence is annoying, really. They look up with glowing eyes, they wag their tails, and some of them even seem to smile. This makes us believe that they truly want our love and admiration, and that these mutual feelings of affection will lead to a satisfactory relationship. What we often fail to overlook, however, is that for all of this love that we think the dog is expressing, the animal actually sees us as no more than a source of food.

Repeated behaviors that elicit positive responses lead to rewards in the form of food. The dog knows only that it is being rewarded for these repeated behaviors, not for real displays of affection. So if I were to give a dog a treat every time it shit on my floor, it would shit on my floor and then look up at me while wagging its tail. It would start pissing on the floor too, to test whether or not that led to a treat. The dog wouldn't do this because it loves me, but because it sees me as a source. Dogs do not love us; they only appear to. You should never forget that I am not a foolish dog owner, and that I do not reward petty behavior."

Jasmine said, "Are you calling me a dog?"

"I never thought that you could be so astute, but yes, I'm calling you a dog. Your groveling display has ruined the grand opening of my restaurant, so I will have no choice but to take it out of your salary."

Jasmine's face contorted with anguish. "Why do you not understand that I am trying to congratulate you? Do you really think that lowly of me, the woman who takes care of your baby?"

Before Fai could utter another response, the foreigner in the green shirt motioned for Jasmine to come to the table. Oblivious of the relationship between the restaurateur and the employee, and assuming that this was a poor woman begging for food from a stranger, he pointed at the untouched bowls of beef chow fun and gestured that he would like to give them to her. Jasmine politely shook her head and refused, but the tourist insisted. He stood up, said hello to the baby that he assumed to be Jasmine's, and guided the pair to the table. He introduced them to the young woman who had a crush on him. Fai's nostrils flared as she looked on.

The young man turned his attention to Fai, made the shape of a box by holding his hands parallel to each other, and said, "Take out?"

Fai put on a fake smile and said, "Yes." She grabbed the bowls of beef chow fun and left the duck, not wanting to be too generous, and went into the kitchen to pack everything up.

By the time she came out, the two foreigners were twiddling their fingers in her baby's face while they cooed. Jasmine smiled at them politely. Fai thought that it was a good thing the maid couldn't speak English, because if she could, she would most likely tell them the truth of the situation. Yes, Fai thought, it was a good thing that this woman was unable to twist the nature of their relationship and present her in an unflattering light. She took umbrage at Jasmine's inability to politely refuse the foreigner's offer, though.

Fai approached her employee with a brown paper bag and gave it to her with arms outstretched and her head cocked to the side. Through a smile, she said, "You have embarrassed me on the biggest day of my life. When you leave the house this Sunday for your day off, don't bother coming back."

Jasmine started to protest, but Fai cut her off.

"If you make a scene right now, things will go really badly for you."

Jasmine put her free hand to her mouth.

Everyone else in the room, except for the foreigners, directed their eyes away from the interaction and back to their food. The foreigner in the green shirt clasped his hands over his chest, and the girl with the bracelets patted him on the back.

"Koeng!" Fai shouted.

"Yes?" Koeng said as he hustled out from the kitchen.

"Walk home with Jasmine and make sure she leaves the baby in the crib. Once she's done that, have her pack her things. If she fails to do any of this, keep her passport."

Koeng began to put a protesting finger up, but brought his hand back down to his side. "Okay. I'll be right back," he said.

Fai nodded.

Without any leverage, Jasmine could only suppress her devastation, accept the leftovers, and thank her now-former employer. Knowing that the tourists had inadvertently exacerbated the situation, she did not acknowledge them before storming out. The bell clinked festively as she left and Koeng followed. With arms akimbo, Fai scanned the restaurant to make an assessment of everyone's expressions. Everyone refused to make eye contact with her.

As they stood at the podium and paid their balance, the tourists exuded an air of exceptionalism. It was clear to Fai that the young man had, in their minds, committed an altruistic act for a lower class woman and her baby. They smiled ignorantly at Fai as she counted out their cash. The lion of the Hong Kong dollar looked proudly into the distance. Fai was sure to address them politely, and when she asked them if their food was delicious, they genuinely answered that it was. After the foreigners exited her restaurant, she breathed a sigh of relief.

At the first opportunity that she had, Fai took the tea-smoked duck into the back office and ate it for lunch. All of her kitchen staff worked in silence as she ate. While Fai tore into the meat and worked it around her mouth, she discovered something that caught her by surprise: it was dry. It did not possess the same rich taste that she had reproduced in tea-smoked duck countless times. By now the moist, smoky richness of the duck came as a reflex of hers, but not this time. Fai was surprised that she had a hard time finishing it. She attributed it to the fact that it had been sitting out for so long, and blamed Jasmine for that. But when she came out of the kitchen to continue her day's work, the restaurant was empty. She took off her apron and draped it over an empty chair, skewed sideways.

The Antipode

As he boarded the tram at Flinders Street Station, Ian gripped the handrail so hard that his knuckles flushed white. After tapping his myki transportation card on the reader, he walked to his seat with his eyes glued to the floor. His lower jaw was set evenly with his upper jaw, and the corners of his lips turned perpetually downward. This gave him the appearance of a frog. The bell clanged as he sat, alerting the pedestrians crossing Swanston Street to clear out.

Ian knew that he had no right to come all the way back to Melbourne. The city itself was too cosmopolitan for him; it offered good food and drink but he thought that it focused too much on catering to hipsters. Ian didn't need the wine bars that served stracciatella. All he wanted was a VB and a meat pie. Apart from the food, Ian thought that the streets themselves had grown to be too fond of hipster sensibilities. The copious amount of what most people called street art was amateurish graffiti. Ian's belief was that if it wasn't in a museum, then it wasn't art, but other people seemed to disagree. These paintings adorned walls in alleys all over the Central Business District, and when Ian arrived in the neighborhood, he saw someone using chalk on the sidewalk.

Not only did Ian dislike Melbourne for its cultural tendencies, but it was the place where he'd gotten dumped one year earlier. It happened in Federation Square, which was across the street from Flinders Street Station, and Chloe hadn't even given him a chance to finish his coffee before shattering his universe. He resented her for that, even now.

In short, he would have preferred to stay away from the city, but he saw no alternative. The day before, Facebook told him that Chloe's fiancé was on a business trip in Brisbane, so he cooked up a scheme to go to their house and win back his ex. The tram crossed over the cocoa-brown Yarra River, leaving the rusted green dome of Flinders Street Station behind it, and Ian wondered whether he was making a good decision.

It took him a moment to warm up from the crisp July air, and while he rubbed his hands together he noticed a young couple sitting across the aisle. The boyfriend had brown hair, and the girlfriend was blonde. Ian thought that she looked like a famous actress, but he couldn't quite put his finger on who she resembled. Movies were not his forte, after all. Either tired or merely affectionate, the girlfriend laid her golden crown on the boyfriend's shoulder, and his black windbreaker swished whenever she shifted her cheek. In seeing a couple like this, Ian felt an intense pang of jealousy. It had only been a year since the last time Chloe had rested her head on his shoulder in the same fashion, yet in that brief window she had already taken concrete steps toward setting up a life with someone else. Ian had to deal with her incessant posts all over social media exhibiting her happiness, watching her embark on adventures she'd never deigned to consider while with him.

On one particular night that she spent over at his place, he told her he wanted to go to New Zealand and try bungee jumping with her, only for her to refuse. She cited the inherent danger in such an activity, and mentioned that she didn't have any proclivity for extreme sports in general. She said that he'd have better luck suggesting the beaches of Bali, but he immediately said that they couldn't go there. Bali was one of her bucket-list destinations, but he couldn't fathom why anyone would take an interest in such a place. He was averse to going there because of the bombings of 2002, and his assumption was that since Indonesia was the most populous Muslim nation on Earth, terrorist attacks were always a risk. Even now, Ian couldn't understand why someone would be afraid of bungee jumping in New Zealand while favoring a trip to Bali. Not going on the bungee trip was one of Ian's biggest regrets of the relationship. To make matters worse, Chloe posted a GoPro video of herself jumping off the ledge at Queenstown just one month after their breakup. This crushed him.

None of the post-breakup travel bothered Ian more than Chloe and her fiancé's recent trip to Amsterdam. They'd gone at the beginning of July, with her posting all of the usual pictures of them doing activities that he'd always wanted to do, like going to a coffeeshop. This also included a post from the Kuala Lumpur airport on the way to Amsterdam, which showcased two bottles of Tiger Beer propped behind two Australian passports. Ian liked the photo in order to get a small measure of revenge that Chloe could think about on the long flight to the Netherlands.

Twelve days later, MH17 bound for Kuala Lumpur from Amsterdam was shot down in eastern Ukraine. Remembering that Chloe's layover had been in the Malaysian capital on the way to Amsterdam, Ian panicked, assuming that she was on the flight. He checked all of her social media and was relieved to see that she had come back to Australia the day before. A picture of Henry — the border collie mix he'd brought home for her one innocuous day two years prior — greeted him on the page.

All of this happened roughly two weeks ago, so reflecting on the occasion overwhelmed Ian. He thought that if he were to strike up a conversation with the couple in front of him, it might take his mind off of it. He looked at the boyfriend across the aisle, locked eyes with him, and said, "How're you going?"

It took the boyfriend a moment to respond, but he said, "I'm doing pretty well."

Ian noticed that this man had an American accent, and while others might consider it rude to bring up nationality so early in a conversation, he didn't have a problem with it. "American. Are you here on holiday?" "Yes, we are."

"It's too bad you came in the dead of winter. Bloody frigid out there."

"We love it in Melbourne," the girlfriend chimed in while keeping her eyes closed. She pronounced the name of the city as "Mel-born."

"*Mel-bn*," Ian corrected her. "I reckon it's much warmer in the States right now."

"We live in Seoul, actually," the boyfriend replied. "But yeah, it's really hot and humid up there right now."

"What are you doing in a place like that? I imagine it's wild."

"We teach English. We love it there," the American said, turning to look at his companion.

"You love it there," she said.

"What's so good about it?" Ian asked.

The American shrugged and said, "Everything in Seoul is convenient. Food is delicious and cheap, there's always stuff to do, and you can travel to other places easily. I think everyone should live abroad at some point, because it challenges you to learn about yourself."

"He's right," the blonde girlfriend said to Ian. She looked at her boyfriend and said, "Well-put. I just don't like spicy food."

"Well that's your problem," the boyfriend said. He pulled his chin back and made a double chin.

The girlfriend laughed and grabbed the bunched up extra skin.

Ian became queasy, because he realized that this seemingly happy couple was only going to make him feel worse. He wished that he could be left to his own devices, but he was already engaged in the conversation. Soldiering on, he asked, "So where are you off to today?"

"St. Kilda," the beau said.

"We've heard good things," the belle added.

"I'm actually headed there myself. Going to see an old friend."

"That's great," the girlfriend said before closing her eyes.

Ian didn't like lying, so he changed the subject. "But St. Kilda is much better in the summer, when it's really going off," he continued. "Even with subpar weather, I recommend the Botanical Gardens. Really great display of the plant life we've got here in Victoria."

"We'll keep that in mind."

The conversation stalled, and Ian was unsure of the reason.

The tram weaved out of the streets of Melbourne and past the Shrine of Remembrance on its way to the southeastern beach suburbs. The tram stopped to pick up new passengers.

The doors let out a hydraulic hiss and a group of teenagers boarded, their heavy footsteps inaudible beneath their chatter. In the mere seconds between boarding and taking their seats in the back of the tram, they must have uttered a dozen curse words. Completely oblivious of their fellow passengers, they carried on their conversation as if no one else was present. They looked to be of Polynesian descent. Ian attempted to trade a look of shared acknowledgement with the couple across from him, but they had moved on to a new conversation in which he was not included. He did not like this isolated state, so he did his best to eavesdrop, but he was unable to glean anything from their conversation because of the teenagers' boisterousness.

He thought about what he would do in the event that he showed up to Chloe's house and she wasn't even home. Leaving a note would not be enough. He thought about breaking in, and knew that Henry wouldn't bark at him. But the house could be fitted with an alarm, and anyone with eyes would be able to see him running away in broad daylight. Maybe he could take a stroll on the beach. Owing to the fact that it was the dead of winter, the place was empty, so a stroll on the shore could be meditative. He could even walk on the pier, a narrow path to nowhere.

He thought about what she might be wearing if she answered the door, and what she might say. Come to think of it, he hadn't yet thought out what *he* would say.

Just as Ian started to think about how he should phrase what he was going to say to his lost love, the teenagers pulled out a portable speaker and put on a rap song on full volume. He tried to ignore it, and while it seemed that the couple across from him was able to tune out the noise, the throbbing bass jostled his brain.

He turned his head to the source of the distraction and said, "Excuse me. Would you mind turning it down, please?"

The teens did not hear him.

"Excuse me."

No response.

Raising his voice, he said, "Could you turn the music down, please?"

This got the teens' attention, but did not yield the result Ian was looking for. One among the group, a raven-haired girl of perhaps sixteen, said, "Fuck off, dickhead."

Ian took this response as an egregious affront. He mustered up enough courage to say, "There are other people on the tram, you know."

"What are you going to do about it?" Said one of the girl's friends, a boy of about 120 kilograms.

Ian had no answer.

"Get stuffed," the girl said. The group kept playing their music, and the conversation they had been conducting before Ian's interruption carried on. The more Ian listened to the adolescents discuss their sexual conquests, shit, and disdain for teachers, the more enraged he became.

Staying on the tram any longer wasn't going to do him any good, so despite Barkly Street being the appropriate stop for Chloe's place, he alighted a stop early at Havelock Street. It was as cold as it had been when he boarded the tram, but the sky was the clearest it had been in weeks. It blended seamlessly with the deep sapphire of the bay, presenting a pristine image of Luna Park, the seaside amusement park. Back in January, Chloe had posted a picture of Luna Park on Instagram in which she was posing in front of the iconic clown-face entrance. The camera was placed strategically enough to give the viewer a downshirt view. The mole on her left breast, which Ian had always said was his favorite mole on her body, was visible. The idea that anyone online could see it enraged him. Unsurprisingly, it was the most liked photo she had posted in months. When Ian sent her a direct message complaining about the post, her reply was, "Mission accomplished."

Heading east on Carlisle Street and internally rehearsing his entreaty to Chloe, Ian spotted a quaint cafe, and suddenly fancied a long black. He figured that going into the establishment would give him more time to scheme, as well as think about what he would do if Chloe were to refuse his advances.

The interior of the cafe, because none of its sixties-era furniture matched, made Ian feel ill at ease. Some of the round salmon tables were paired with a mix of plastic sea green and orange chairs, but higher blue tables also had a sea green chair and a white chair paired. Some tables were round, and some were rectangular. The levels of the tables were uneven, and all of this caused Ian's skin to grow itchy. He didn't like disorder. The restaurant was mostly empty, however, with only a few other patrons seated at these strangely configured pieces of furniture. Ian wanted to get his long black as quickly as possible and leave.

This proved difficult for him, however, as the barista took forever to make his beverage.

She ground the coffee with a manual grinder, and he could hear the beans crunch one by one. After three minutes of this, she went into the back room and brought out a portafilter, only to find that it was dirty. She went to the back room again, returned with a clean portafilter, and delicately poured the grounds into it. She tamped down the grounds as gently as if they were piled on top of a sleeping baby's head, and brought them to the machine. She struggled to latch the portafilter on, and the metal slid and clacked as she made her attempt. Ian tapped his foot as he waited.

When Ian finally received the long black, he discovered that it actually tasted quite good.

It had a light amount of the caramel-colored foam that he thought to be indicative of a quality long black, and it was characterized by rich caramel and chocolate notes. Drinking it afforded him greater clarity in organizing his thoughts. However, some of his agitation remained because of the unsettling furniture, as well as how long the barista had taken to prepare the beverage.

Ian kept his ex-girlfriend's address, acquired from her Facebook page without her knowledge, in the Notes section of his phone. A cool breeze swept off the bay as he entered it into his map application. While he had his phone out, he looked at Chloe's Instagram. Nothing to report on today, but he scrolled down the page to look at the older pictures. Having his head buried in his phone caused Ian to not notice a major obstacle: the Polynesian teenagers from the tram. He didn't even notice that they were still blaring rap on their stereo.

They saw him first and quickened their pace toward him. Before Ian was able to walk away from them, the group surrounded him.

"Oy, dipstick," the black-haired girl said.

Ian looked around at all of their faces and said, "Can I help you?"

"We didn't like the way you talked to us on the tram," the girl said.

Even in this situation, Ian's mind returned to the idea of Chloe being on MH17. Now he saw the teenagers as a greater irritant. He said, "Well I don't like your attitude, you disrespectful little mongrel."

"Mind your own business."

"I've been trying to come up with my plan all day, and all you've been doing is nagging at me like a baby that just shat its pants."

"What are you talking about?" the large boy said.

Ian kept his eyes fixed on the girl's eyes and said, "This is our last chance to be together, and if you turn me down, I'll never get a chance to be happy. Why can't you see that this is what's best?"

"This bogan's gone apeshit," the girl said.

Irate at this accusation, Ian threw his long black in the teenage girl's face. She shrieked in pain as the brew seared her skin like an ahi steak.

With that, the mob of teenagers was on Ian, engulfing him in a swirl of kicks and punches that knocked him to the ground. He curled up and covered his head, but that didn't prevent anything. They kicked his ribs, punched his kidneys, and one of them even kicked him in the face. The pain was excruciating, and he could taste the blood where his incisor used to be. The gang continued to pound him mercilessly, and pretty soon all of the agony throughout his body dovetailed into one vast expanse of pain.

Ian's vision was blurred when he awoke, but the sterile white walls, rough linen sheets, and smell of iodine allowed him to ascertain that he was in a hospital. More importantly, he saw a female figure standing at the foot of his bed, and the way she stood with her elbow cradled in her left hand told him that it was Chloe. The sight of her, no matter how agitated she appeared to be, made him want to get out of the bed and hug her.

He groaned to get her attention, licked his cracked lips, and said, "You came."

"You listed me as your emergency contact, so I felt like I had no choice."

"It means that you still care about me."

"No, Ian, it doesn't. It means that I wanted to see you at rock bottom."

"What?"

Chloe ignored his confusion and said, with a smirk, "Why were you so close to our house?"

He hated the way she said *our*. "After thinking you were on that flight, I wanted to see you." A shock of pain reverberated through his ribs. He winced.

"That's nice of you Ian, but you need to get it through your head that we're done. I can't have you coming around the house when my fiance is out of town. It's not good for either of us."

"Chloe."

"You've got to get over it. Maybe you can start by unfollowing all of my pages." Ian tried to clench his jaw, but couldn't because of the pain.

She laughed. "If you don't do it, I'll block you."

Ian said, "Did you go bungee jumping and go to Amsterdam because you wanted to make me —"

She interrupted him. "For the final year of us being together, you lorded over every aspect of our relationship, from our future plans to what we would eat for dinner. You never once asked me about what I wanted out of life, or even about my days at work. Now you want to be nice to me because you thought for a second that I was in a plane crash?" While she said this, she scratched her ear. The ring glimmered in the fluorescent light.

He started, "Can't you see that we are perfect —"

"Shut up, already."

He started to cry.

She said, "Ugh. Don't embarrass yourself." She walked out, her heels clacking on the floor.

After Chloe was gone, Ian tried to go back to sleep, but it did not come easy. The harder he tried, the less easily it came to him. He attempted to breathe deeply and relax his muscles but his mind was running at far too active a pace for him to get the rest he needed. As he lay there thinking about everything that had transpired, from the lacerations at the hands of the teenage gang to the laceration suffered at the hands of Chloe, he realized once and for all that he didn't have a future with Chloe. Forlorn, he buzzed the nurse in order to ask her for morphine, and he hoped that she would give him enough to make him sleep not just now, but forever.

Ping Pong

For most of the people who walked in this area, it was their first night in Bangkok.

Naiyana sat on the barstool, crossing the high heel on her right foot over her left leg. She was a striking young woman, with hair as black as a Jack Daniel's label. It contrasted with her chestnut skin beautifully. She wore a skin-tight red dress that prioritized fashion over comfort, and she'd applied lipstick to match. The sidewalk bar, a stall set up in the same fashion as a street food cart, was empty save for a couple of other girls working and the bartender, a glowering young man who watched her every move. Everything, from the thatched roof to the colored lanterns, was set up to try to lure customers in as they ambled out of Sukhumvit Station, but the lights and pristinely polished bottles of assorted liquor didn't have quite the pull that Soi Cowboy did. The bar was a sort of pilot fish to the shark that was Soi Cowboy, catching the runoff of those heading to the bikini-clad women, neon signs, and ping pong shows of the famous street. It was a jungle in there, a jungle that Naiyana had always sought to avoid. Now that she was working just outside of it, exploiting its draw, she felt that she was becoming part of the machine. The red lights of the infamous alley, spilling out onto the sidewalk like water from a broken levee, bathed her profile as she sat and waited.

A young Western man tentatively approached the bar. The other girls called to him and told him to sit down, but he sat down on the barstool next to Naiyana instead. He ordered two gin and tonics and set down ten five-hundred baht notes. While the bartender prepared the cocktails, the young man crossed his arms, leaned on the bar, and looked at Naiyana out of the corner of his eye. The bartender pulled up the corners of his lips in a fake smile as he set the glasses down and swiped only one of the bills that the patron had set on the bar. Gin spilled over one of the glasses, dampening the cocktail napkin beneath it.

The young man chuckled as he pulled back the remaining nine bills. "I can never get the conversion rate right," he said to himself. He turned to Naiyana and said, "My name is Sean," extending his hand. "I hope you like gin and tonic, or as they call it in Korea, 'gin tonic.'"

"Nice to meet you," Naiyana said as she brought the gin and tonic to her lips. "My name is Cherry."

"Ooh, I like cherries. They're sweet."

"That's good. If you like real cherries, then you will like me."

Sean laughed. "I like that attitude," he said. "So do you live around here?"

"Yeah, not too far." She hoped that he wouldn't ask her any personal questions, like whether or not she had siblings, or if she had kids. That was always the worst. "Is this your first time in Bangkok?"

Sean gulped his gin and tonic, and the ice cubes clacked together as Naiyana waited for his response. He set the glass down and said, "It is," before taking another moment to chew the ice cubes in his mouth. "I'm only here for two nights before I fly to Mandalay, though."

"I've heard that city is a wasteland. Why wouldn't you go to Mandalay Bay instead?"

He laughed. "Believe me, Mandalay Bay isn't that great."

"I wish I could go to Las Vegas. It looks so glamorous."

He shook his head as he took a sip. "Going there one time is cool, but you don't need to go there much after that. I'd rather go somewhere like Mandalay — a place with some culture."

"I only want to go one time."

He shrugged and said, "Fair enough."

"You make Mandalay sound good. I could come with you, if you like," she said.

Sean took another gulp of his gin and tonic and ordered another. "Sure, why not. You're cute enough," he said with a smile.

Naiyana knew this was lip service, but that didn't stop her from inwardly rejoicing the fact that she would not be ditched for the more outwardly lascivious women down the alley. At least not for the time being. "What do you do for work?" She asked her client, knowing by now that this question was a common conversation starter among Americans.

"I teach English to kids in Seoul," he said as he grabbed his new glass. "It's not the best job, but at least I get to travel. Living in a different country is the best kind of travel that you can do."

"Why?"

He took a healthy swig that included ice. "It's not like going to a resort somewhere and relaxing on the beach. For me, the real adventure is in daily life, when you're confronted with difficulties in what would normally be easy."

"That doesn't sound very fun," Naiyana said. "Why not just go somewhere and meet a beautiful woman?"

He grinned and shook his head. "It's hard to explain," he said.

Naiyana thought it was hard to listen to, so she asked, "Do you know where you will go on your next trip?"

"Not totally sure yet. Maybe Bali. I heard it's cool there."

"I've heard good things about Bali. You should go there," Naiyana said with a giggle. "And you should take me with you."

"I thought we were already going to Mandalay together," he said.

"I changed my mind. I want Bali," she responded, putting her hand on his knee.

He went on to have two more drinks after that, while she managed not only to finish hers, but have a second as they talked about everything from orangutans in Borneo to business school programs in the United States. Even with the drinks, Naiyana grew bored with Sean's company. The more drinks he had, the more he pontificated. It did not help Naiyana foster a faux attraction to him.

When the time came, she leaned in close to his ear, and with a whisper almost as muggy as the dense night air, suggested that they head to a love motel. He countered that the two of them not only head to the love motel, but that they walk through Soi Cowboy first. She didn't want to go through the famous red-light alley, but didn't want to lose his interest.

The red lights shot out at the couple and pulled them in like flies on a chameleon's tongue. Women were everywhere, beckoning to any man who passed them. As Naiyana and Sean walked past the first go-go bars on the street and visions of other women writhing to music bursting through open doors, Naiyana slid her left index finger into one of Sean's belt loops. It was a move to which he did not object. Her job was not to patronize another bar with this man, but to get him to the designated love motel as soon as possible and finish what she had set out to do. Taking him into a bar would run the risk of him running off with another woman, and all of her efforts would have been for nought.

She led him through Soi Cowboy, her finger remaining hooked to him the entire time. Various women and ladyboys tried to lure him into bars with Siren songs such as, "Hey big boy," "I want to play," and "You like pussy?"

One of the women smacked her lips to make a popping sound. Then she said, "You want to come to a ping pong show? Ping pong, chopping bananas, releasing doves, and blowing darts!" She resumed smacking her lips, but added a crotch grab.

Naiyana worked hard to steer Sean away from this one.

Another woman, wearing little more than a cowboy hat and boots, wielded a bottle of tequila and attempted to pour its contents down the gullet of any and all male passersby. Her eyes, upon closer inspection, were absent of any cogency; she'd clearly nipped a hefty amount of the liquor herself, but whether she did so because it was fun or because she didn't want to remember where her night was headed was unclear. Naiyana was unable to veer Sean away from this dead-eyed temptress, as he ended up taking two shots with the cowgirl and putting his arm around her. The woman reached for his crotch, but Naiyana anticipated the move and beat her to it. This was the only way for Naiyana to extricate him.

After only a few steps away from the cowgirl, Sean saw the neon placard for a go-go bar and went straight for the entrance. Naiyana had no choice but to follow him in.

Two large men in black t-shirts stood at the interior entrance. Beyond them was a stage fitted with poles and nearly thirty women dancing on it. Each of the women had a numbered slip of paper attached to their bikini bottom. Hot tubs surrounded the stage, a few of which already had customers in them.

One of the men asked, "Are you looking for a girl?"

Sean brought his attention from the tubs to the man and began to nod, but Naiyana cut him off and said, "No." She pulled on him, but he resisted. Once again, the only way to extricate him was to grab his crotch.

Two 7-Elevens opposite each other stood outside of the love motel. The motel itself was an inconspicuous building, intentionally designed for patrons to clandestinely slip in and out to commit whatever unsavory act they desired. The only characteristic giving the building away as a love motel was a curtain drawn across the door for the sake of secrecy. Otherwise, it would have appeared to be any other undistinguished apartment building. When he saw it, Sean complained to Naiyana that he wanted more girls. She forced him through the front entrance.

The pair walked through a narrow corridor to the lobby, which was unlike that of a standard hotel. The lobby was a small, dimly-lit red-carpeted room with a slot in the wall. It was as if a ticket window had been made with drywall instead of glass. Instead of movie tickets, patrons received their room keys from the slot. In Thai, Naiyana instructed the employee to give them a key. She then switched to English to ask Sean for five hundred baht, then back to Thai to finish the transaction. She took the key from the slot and headed for the elevator.

They only had to go to the second floor, but Naiyana preferred the elevator to the stairs. Safer for someone in Sean's state. The corridor on the second floor was darker than the inside of a closet. As they got closer to their destination, Sean got increasingly grabby. Since his drunkenly floppy hand wasn't accomplishing much, Naiyana humored him. After a few moments of what Sean probably thought passed for foreplay,

Naiyana found the room, inserted the key into the lock, and opened the door.

When Sean saw the inside of the room, he immediately burst into laughter. The walls were lined with three-dimensionally contoured Popeye characters. Bluto was just to the left of the door, shaking his fist at Popeye and Olive Oyl on the opposite wall. They were standing at the bow of the boat jutting out slightly over the bed. Olive Oyl was laying smooches on Popeye's cheeks. Everything else in the room, in order to establish a nautical theme in line with the Popeye characters, was white with navy trim. This included the rest of the walls, the floor, the bedding, and everything in the bathroom. Barring the condoms next to the sink, the room looked like it belonged at Disneyland. Naiyana went to the bathroom and left Sean to his own devices.

While Sean should have been stripping and helping himself to one of the condoms, he walked up to Popeye and Olive Oyl and snapped a selfie, giggling like a girl reading her rival's diary. Naiyana came out of the bathroom naked, and stopped when she saw what Sean was doing.

"Have you been to a love motel before?"

He put his phone in his pocket, knowing better than to keep the possibility of snapping a photo of her present. He looked at her nude, slender frame, and was clearly not accustomed to such a body. It was almost as if he had never seen a grown woman naked before. He refused to bring his eyes to hers. She stood, arms akimbo.

"Have you?"

He snapped out of his trance. "No, I haven't. They have them in Korea, but I haven't been in one."

"Well, it's fifteen hundred. Leave it on the counter and get undressed. One hour."

Sean counted out the money and laid it down before scrambling to pull his cargo shorts off. Naiyana slinked onto the bed, just under Popeye's boat. Sean walked over to the sink and tore one of the condoms away from the others before struggling to open it. His hands were too sweaty; his fingers kept slipping off of the wrapper. Naiyana sighed, grabbed the remote, and turned on the TV. The first image to appear was a couple having sex in a shower. She hoped that he wouldn't ask her to try that.

"Do you want to try that?" he asked.

Just what she didn't want. "Okay," she said, pulling herself off of the bed.

She grabbed the condom wrapper out of his hand, ripped it open, and placed the condom in his palm before walking into the bathroom. She stepped into the shower and turned on the water.

Before the water warmed up, Sean noticed the whirlpool. "They have a Jacuzzi in here?!" he said in disbelief. "I thought I missed my chance at the go-go bar, but I guess not. Let's do it in here instead."

She was fine with that for a couple of reasons. First, she didn't like having sex in the shower because she didn't like doing it while standing. Second, the whirlpool required them to draw water first, which would bite into the time she was allotting Sean.

"Yes, we can do that. I think that would be sexier." She walked to the whirlpool, drew the water, and put a hand on Sean's thigh.

He said, "So about before, when you mentioned that you wanted to come with me to Mandalay, that might not be able to happen."

Naiyana snorted. "It's just a fun joke, you know," she said as she worked her hand toward his dick.

"There's something that I think I should tell you."

"Don't tell me you're a virgin."

"No. It's not that. I have a girlfriend, and she's actually here in Bangkok with me. She complains a lot, which is annoying. Now she's sick, and it's dragging the trip down. I'm sorry I lied to you."

"I don't care," she said, as she continued to work listlessly. "Most of the men I work with are married."

"Can you not talk about the other men that you work with," he said. "It makes me uncomfortable."

"Okay."

A moment passed and he said, "Do you want to go to a ping pong show with me after we're done?"

"That's not part of my job," she said.

The whirlpool was properly drawn, so Naiyana pressed the button that activated the jets.

Water bubbled up to the surface, and the tub took on the appearance of a boiling witch's cauldron. Stepping into it wouldn't suck her soul out of her, however. In that moment, she felt that she'd already lost her soul years earlier.

"Come on in," Sean said, slipping both legs into the tub and sliding into a seated position. "The water's fine."

Naiyana, knowing from watching American movies that this line was banal, joined her client in the tub. As soon as her foot hit the surface, Sean grabbed her. He laughed and moved his hands all over like a mime pretending to wrestle an octopus. By applying downward pressure, he signaled that he wanted her to sit down on his lap, facing away from him. Once she did, and the warm water reached her chest, he put himself inside her. Without any nuance or grace, he started to thrust. Naiyana hoped that it would end soon, and focused on the image of Bluto shaking his fist on the bedroom wall.

Against Naiyana's hopes, Sean was having trouble. He apologized profusely and continued to fumble around, but nothing changed. She stood up and told him to do the same so that she could go down on him, but he said no. When she looked at him, he had an impish look on his face.

"I have a better idea," he said.

"What?"

"Why don't you run to the 7-Eleven downstairs and get some ping pong balls? I'll give you a couple extra baht."

She hesitated for a moment, but said yes.

The water whooshed as he stood up. He got out of the tub, toweled himself off, and walked over to his cargo shorts crumpled on the floor. Naiyana got out of the tub and prepared to go back out.

Sean handed her a handful of coins. "This should be enough."

"Thank you," she said, without looking at the money.

"Hurry up," he said as he walked over to the bed. "I'll be waiting."

While his back was turned, Naiyana took the money off the counter and left.

Naiyana had no intention of going to 7-Eleven. When she was in the hallway, she counted the money, and it came out to 15,000 baht. For every 100 baht Sean thought he gave her, he actually gave 1,000. She broke out in a smile and quickened her pace as she stuffed the money into her bra. She couldn't wait for the elevator, and by the time she reached the stairs, she was in a full-on sprint. The sound of her heels echoed in the imitation marble stairwell.

After exiting the hotel, Naiyana took her shoes off and ran through Soi Cowboy. The pavement was smooth and warm under her feet, and the crowd of women was thinner by this time. Despite this, she still had to juke constantly in order to avoid a collision. Right when she thought she was going to make it out clean, the drunken cowgirl from earlier stumbled into her path. Naiyana did what she could to avoid her, but it wasn't enough. She slammed into her at full speed, and both women went down to the pavement. The tequila bottle flew out of the woman's hand and shattered on the sidewalk. This drew everyone's attention in the area, and a crowd gathered.

Naiyana checked her bra. The money was still there. The cowgirl swore at her and tried to grab her hair, but Naiyana swatted the woman's hand away easily. As she pressed herself up, however, she heard Sean shout, "Hey!" from the direction of the love motel.

She stood up and started to run, but as soon as she took her first step she felt a shard of glass dig into her right heel. She winced and sucked air through her gritted teeth. While she wanted to take a look at her wound, she didn't have time. She tried her best to pry her way through the crowd, but they would not give her an opening. Some accused Naiyana of attacking the cowgirl and called for a fight. Sean's shouts grew louder as Naiyana wedged herself between two smaller women. It turned out the crowd wasn't as bloodthirsty as much as it was merely entertainment-thirsty, so Naiyana was finally able to break free of them before the cowgirl got to her feet.

Some in the crowd attended to the cowgirl, who bled from her scraped elbow, and others dispersed. Sean bounced outside of the expanding circle and trailed Naiyana, gaining ground with each step. Naiyana ran on her tiptoes, carried her shoes in one hand, and held the money to her chest with the other.

Sean yelled, "Give me my money!"

Judging by the volume of his voice, Naiyana guessed that he was only a few meters behind her. She saw the bar at the end of Soi Cowboy and reached her fingers into her bra. Right when she felt Sean's fingers grasp for her hair, she made eye contact with the bartender. Naiyana must have looked as frightened as the bartender had ever seen her, because he rushed out to stop Sean. Just as Sean was about to grab a fistful of hair, the bartender stepped in front of him and leaned his shoulder into him. Sean fell onto his back.

Naiyana scurried behind the now-empty bar and watched. The bartender stood over Sean, who grimaced and was rubbing his shoulder.

"I have the money," she called out to the bartender.

"Leave it on the bar," he said without taking his eyes off Sean.

"She stole that money from me," Sean said to the bartender. "I only meant to pay her the regular rate, but she has way more than that."

The bartender didn't understand English. All he said to Sean was, "No."

To the bartender, Naiyana said, "I'm giving you a little extra because you helped me." She pulled the entire stack of bills out of her bra and counted them.

While Naiyana was counting, Sean pointed at her and said, "Look! Look at how much money she has!"

But the bartender's gaze did not waver. To Naiyana, he said, "Thank you."

Naiyana set down 2,000 baht, put the rest of the money back in her bra, and headed to Asok Station.

When she got to the station, she hurried up the steps, tapped her transit card on the way to the platform, and waited for the train. She kept her eyes active while she waited, making sure that Sean hadn't somehow stalked behind her. The train arrived, screeching healthily to a halt.

Naiyana looked over both shoulders, confirmed that Sean hadn't made it to the station, and entered the train.

The train was practically empty, operating at the late hour that it was. Naiyana was grateful for this fact as she slumped onto the yellow plastic bench. The seat, contoured to accommodate a person's backside, cradled Naiyana as she let her concerns about Sean pursuing her fade away. She had the money, after all, and was on her way home.

Naiyana took this opportunity to take a look at the glass in her foot. It was a small shard, no larger than a pomegranate seed. She figured that it would bleed if she took it out, so she left it. She let her foot drop slowly to the floor, felt the money on her chest, and breathed a sigh of relief. Looking around at the handful of other people in that particular car with her, she tried to imagine what they had all been through that evening, and whether or not the events compared to hers. Only one of them stood out above the others.

Sitting to Naiyana's right, in a red dress similar to her own, was a ladyboy. The ladyboy held her bag in the crux of her elbow while her smartphone rested in perfectly manicured hands. Naiyana imagined that she had been out, possibly even in Soi Cowboy, looking for a date. She hadn't been looking for a date in the way that Naiyana had, but rather in a way that would provide her with some companionship. The ladyboy must have felt Naiyana's eyes on her, as she looked up from her phone and at Naiyana. Her downcast eyes betrayed a deep sense of loneliness and inadequacy.

Naiyana felt connected to this ladyboy, in that they'd both been chewed up by the shadows of the Bangkok night, but were able to escape before being completely devoured. For while it was late, it was not yet the part of night in which the truly horrible acts were committed. For a brief moment, before alighting at Pra Khanong Station, Naiyana considered giving the ladyboy some of the money that Sean had mistakenly paid her, but ultimately decided against it. Instead, she got off the train, went home, and looked for the first aid kit.

Headless Buddha

It had been four years since Myanmar opened itself up to the rest of the world, but Jojo was still working to figure out how to see the wealth coming in. He didn't live particularly close to the Bagan Archaeological Area like many of the people he knew, and wasn't able to acquire souvenirs from distributors as easily, so he didn't have many advantages when it came to making a living as a peddler. What he did have, however, was a temple in his backyard.

The baked clay temple towered over a clearing surrounded by lush green trees, and served as the only landmark in sight. Jojo's temple was set away from the thousands of temples, pagodas, and stupas of Bagan, but that did not mean that it was any less majestic. A ribbed spire projected from its bulbous dome into the sky, and the six additional spires flanking the dome on terraces provided an ethereal symmetry. This temple, oddly enough, did not appear on any postcards available at nearby Nyaung U Airport or elsewhere. This might have been because of its location, but it was more likely because of Jojo's house being so close to it. Ananda Temple, with its narrow, golden dome, did not have a corrugated tin shack in front of it. Because of this, as well as its central location, it had a makeshift market inside of it and was arguably the most recognizable temple in Myanmar. Anyone looking to make a day's salary by selling off a sand painting or a bootleg copy of George Orwell's *Burmese Days* knew that it was best to camp out in places such as Ananda.

As Jojo listened to the metallic patter of rain on his roof, he packed a fresh chaw of betel in his mouth and watched the trees gently sway in the wind. With every raindrop, the footprints in the clay mud began to transform into puddles opaque with sediment. While one puddle near Jojo was rippling, he spit a stream of saliva maroon with betel juice into it and watched it grow dark. The putter of a motorbike snapped Jojo's attention away from the puddle and to a newfound opportunity.

Two foreign tourists entered the temple grounds, one male and one female. They both wore helmets, which meant that they'd rented one of the motorbikes from whichever hotel they were staying at. What Jojo assumed to be the wife had her arms crossed and her brows furrowed. On a clear day, Jojo might have been able to hear their conversation from this distance, but the sound of the rain prevented that today. The husband walked tall and wore a curious grin on his face, but Jojo guessed that if the wife wasn't happy, then getting them to go inside the temple was going to be a tough sell. It had been a couple of days since he'd last had any foreign visitors, so regardless of what he took to be a poor forecast, he had to try to get them to go in.

Jojo twisted the sparse hairs on his chin as he watched the couple walk toward the opposite side of the temple. The husband's gait wavered a bit, and he tried to put his arm around his companion's waist. Before his fingers could settle on her hip bone, she pulled his hand off and shoved it away. The couple vanished from Jojo's view as they began their circuit around the temple. Once they had fully disappeared, Jojo went over to his son Khin, who slept on a bed behind him, and jostled him awake. The boy, barely older than tourism in Myanmar, moaned groggily. The family chicken clucked near the foot of the bed.

"Get the flashlight," Jojo told him.

"Why?" Khin asked, rolling away from his father.

"You know why."

"I don't want to go," the boy said, sitting up.

"You have to go," Jojo said. "Tourists trust children more than adults. If they see you first, they might actually agree to go into the temple. Okay?"

Khin rubbed the rheum from his eyes and said, "Okay."

"Good. Get your longyi on."

Khin stepped out of bed and reached between the paint brushes and stack of paintings on the table between him and his father to grab the long blue and green plaid skirt crumpled up on the table. He beat the dust off and snapped it in front of him to straighten out the wrinkles before stepping into the center of the cloth cylinder and hiking it up to the top of his hip bones. Khin deftly grabbed the excess cloth of the longyi and tied a knot in the front. Jojo smiled and approached his son.

"Remember: be cute."

"I don't like being cute."

"I know you don't." Jojo said as he moved behind his son. "But tourists like it." He grabbed Khin's shoulders and leaned in so that they could watch the temple together. While they waited for the tourists to round the last corner, Jojo rubbed Khin's shoulders.

The tourists emerged at the far right corner of Jojo's field of vision. They walked along the outer wall of the temple, with a distance between them that Jojo would not consider intimate. They walked slowly and with their heads down, failing to enjoy the beautiful scenery. The way they carried themselves discouraged Jojo, and if he had been visited by tourists more that month, he would have called off the plan.

Knowing that this was not the case, he said, "When do you approach them?"

"When they get to the secret entrance."

"Not bad, son, but no. You want to go just before they get to the secret entrance, because it will take time to run over there, and they might continue walking after you greet them."

"Okay."

"Don't worry. You're getting better."

The couple got close to the secret entrance of the temple. Jojo worried that their shoe gazing would lead to them missing it, because it was no more than a small hole above a ledge, a meter and a half off the ground. The wife, however, looked up at the appropriate moment, grabbed her husband by the arm, and pointed the hole out to him. This was the opportunity Jojo had been waiting for, and he acted accordingly.

He said, "Do you have the flashlight?"

Khin held it up, and Jojo gave him a gentle push.

The boy jogged to the foreigners, at the non-threatening pace that he had practiced with his father, and approached the couple. The red-clay puddles splashed at his heels as his ran, and he made sure that he entered their sight through their periphery. That way, they were not too startled by his approach. Jojo watched the couple turn away from the entrance and toward his son, who presented them with the flashlight. Jojo had taught Khin to greet tourists by using the English phrase, "Hello! Want to go in?" It was at this moment that he should have been uttering this to the couple. Jojo watched as Khin gave the tourists a spread-fingered wave. The couple did not give the boy a negative reaction. Jojo saw the wife grab the husband by the arm, but not in a defensive manner. It was then that Jojo decided that he would enter himself into the interaction. Khin's work was done.

The couple was busy trying to talk to the young boy when Jojo walked up to them with a smile on his face. He arrived at the stone walkway surrounding the temple and waved to them. He patted Khin on the shoulder, took the flashlight from him, and, switching to English, said, "I see you met my son. Do you want to go in?" Khin giggled and ran back to their house.

The husband raised an eyebrow and said, "In where?"

The wife rolled her eyes and said, "In the temple."

"Oh. Why would we want to go in there?" the boyfriend asked, sloppily motioning to the little black gap.

"I don't know," she said, before turning to Jojo. "What's in there?" She asked.

Jojo said, "There is a Buddha in there that is eight hundred years old." He knelt down, and with his finger drew an imaginary square route. He said, "We go in, and go through the temple like this, before getting to the Buddha. It will take twenty minutes."

The couple thought in silence for a moment, and the wife said, "Let's do it."

"No. I don't want to go in," the husband said. "I'm too drunk for that."

"I told you to lay off those Myanmar Beers at lunch," the wife said.

"How could I?" the husband said, defensively. "Six of those big mugs cost like four dollars."

The wife crossed her arms, shook her head, and said, "Whatever. We never do anything *spontranible* anymore." Jojo wasn't sure of what the long "s" word meant. His English wasn't perfect, and long words sometimes gave him trouble. Whatever the word was, it set the husband off and caused an argument to erupt between them. The couple was speaking too quickly and angrily for Jojo to be able to keep up, so he simply stood there with his arms behind his back and hoped that they would end up deciding to go into the temple.

After a few moments of going back and forth, the wife turned to Jojo and said, "I'll go in."

Jojo said, "Really?" He motioned to the husband. "Is he coming?"

"Nope," she said. "He doesn't need to."

The wife took off her helmet and handed it to the husband. If he was being honest with himself, Jojo was relieved. One less person inside the temple made things easier for him. After the wife was ready, Jojo climbed up onto the ledge and led her through the narrow entrance into the pitch black interior.

Jojo landed on the old brick walkway inside. The footing was uneven, and he extended his hand to the wife to support her. She did not take his hand. When they were both inside, they noticed that the patter of the rain was absent. It was like a sound booth. The light from the outside only seeped in a meter or two, so Jojo turned on the flashlight.

There was a pungent smell of mildew. Jojo explained that there were bats, but that there was no reason to fear them because they did not bite. Usually when Jojo explained this to tourists, it spooked them a little bit, but this particular woman found it amusing, and that took him by surprise.

As they penetrated the darkness, the brick walkway dissipated into sand, and their feet sank into it. Jojo knew that like just about anything in Bagan, the sand was red. After a short time walking straight ahead in silence, and only following the beam of light, the wife said,

"What's it like to live in Myanmar?"

"We live a quiet life here, but I like it."

"I don't want to offend you about this, but I'm curious: What do you think of the Rohingya?"

Jojo said, "They do not exist."

"I'm sorry."

"Do not worry. There is bad news about Burma."

About a minute later, she said, "I'm sorry about him."

"Who?"

"The guy I came with."

"It is okay," Jojo said over his shoulder. "Most people do not want to see the Buddha."

"I think he thought it was dangerous," the wife stated, laughing nervously.

"There is nothing to worry about," Jojo said, spitting a red stream into the sand. They arrived at a wall. They had to boost themselves up onto a ledge and crawl through a gap smaller than the one they'd crawled through when they'd entered. Jojo set the flashlight on the ledge so that it illuminated the girl's path. He gripped the bottom lip of the hole — sticky with guano — boosted himself up, then crawled through the gap and turned around to monitor her progress. It was the first time that he had really taken a good look at her. He thought she was beautiful. Her blonde hair flowed down to her shoulders, and even though it was wet, it looked more lustrous than any hair he had seen before. He thought that she could just have easily been the actress from the *The Italian Job*, which had been on TV the previous week. He decided he should tell her that.

"You look like that actress from *The Italian Job*. I don't know her name."

"Who? Charlize Theron?" She laughed while stepping on a stone and wiggling her foot to make sure it was stable. "No I don't."

"You do."

"Well, thank you." She boosted herself up to the gap. In order to make sure he wasn't uncomfortably close to her, Jojo grabbed the flashlight and backed away. He kept the light on the gap so that she could see where she was going. After she had squeezed herself through and brought herself back down to path level, he proceeded onward.

It was then that the first bats flew by. They were little white fur balls, and the gentle "pfft pfft pfft" sound of their wings as they flapped was the only sound they made. The wife remarked on how cute they were, and said that it was a surprise that the bats did not squeak.

Once they had another opportunity to speak, the wife asked Jojo, "How do you know where to go in here?"

"I learned from my father. And he learned from his father. My family has lived in front of this temple since before the war, but we could only go in after the Japanese blew open that hole. Before that — for over seven hundred years — it was sealed off from everybody."

"That's amazing," she replied.

"Yes," Jojo affirmed. He worked his tongue between his teeth. One of them wobbled.

The two of them continued on, following the beam from the flashlight in silence. The light was a knife into the darkness, wedging into the bricks that had been set there by Jojo's ancestors. Jojo wondered what it had been like inside the temple when nobody could enter.

Myanmar was always rife with internal conflict. The Pagan Kingdom had built this temple when they became the first to unify Myanmar, but was later conquered by the Yuan dynasty. Eventually the British came, and finally the Japanese blew the temple open. Even after the temple was opened up, infighting continued during the junta and up to the present day. And although Jojo didn't believe they existed, the Rohingya were currently being forced out of their homes in Rakhine State.

With all of this in mind (except for the Rohingya), Jojo reflected that life on the outside of the temple was not much different now than how it had been in the past, but in the past the inside of the temple was isolated from the corruption of the outside world. This was probably how the Buddha liked it, as he simply sat alone in the grand structure, shrouded in darkness.

There was one more gap that they had to crawl through, and this one led into the most popular chamber for the bats. Knowing that the wife would appreciate seeing the bats hanging from the ceiling, Jojo shined the light up at them after they had gotten back to their feet. The bats were little fuzzy onions on the ceiling, and while the draft emanating from the entrance of the temple was barely perceptible, it made them swing. Contrary to Jojo's expectations, the wife did not have much of a reaction to the bats. He guessed that seeing them so clearly made her uncomfortable.

"They are friendly bats," Jojo reassured her. "They do not bite."

"Yeah, I know. You said that before."

After a moment of uncomfortable silence, Jojo said, "We are close."

At long last, the two of them reached the Buddha. If he hadn't told her that they had arrived, she most likely would not have noticed the statue. It stood there in an arched enclave dug into the wall on the right, about one-and-a-half meters tall. The Buddha was solitary and shorter than the tourist had probably expected. The most surprising attribute, however, was that the little marble statue was headless.

"Why does he have no head?" the wife asked.

"When the Japanese came to Burma, they wanted to kill the culture. So they cut off his head."

"Don't they have Buddhism in Japan?"

"Yes, but it is different. We have Theravada here, and that is not the same." Jojo said. He gestured to the statue. "Take a look at him."

The wife leaned down and brought her face to the stump of a neck. Jojo angled the flashlight so that she could observe it more closely. She reached her hand up to the shoulder, and ran a finger across the worn curves. Jojo didn't particularly like the way that she was touching the Awakened One, but he was learning that curiosity often got the best of tourists. The more acquainted the wife became with the Buddha, observing the contours in the carved robe and the weathered hands melting into the body, the more drawn in she became. Her breath grew deeper every second, and her motions drew slower. Her eyes worked their way down the smaller-than-advertised relic, eventually reaching the temple floor. Tears dribbled out of her eyes and onto the sand, dying it crimson. Jojo didn't say a word, afraid that he might upset her further. She sniffled, wiped her nose with her forearm, and stood up.

"Will you take my picture?"

"Sure," Jojo said, extending his hand for her phone.

She prepared the phone and handed it to him. "I turned the flash on. Is that okay?"

"Yes, that is fine," Jojo said. "Thank you for asking."

Jojo took a couple of pictures of her crouched down with the Buddha, but no matter how many pictures he took of her, her face was unable to express joy. He didn't want to keep her down on the ground for too long, so he said the picture was good and handed the camera back to her.

She looked at the picture and sniffled, "This is incredible. Thank you for bringing me in here."

"I like to do it," Jojo said, unsure of how to reply to this kind reaction.

"Well, thank you," she said?

Jojo felt pang of curiosity for this girl's story. "I did not ask, but where are you from?"

"America. I'm from Chicago, and my boyfriend is from California," she said.

"Boyfriend? You two are not married?"

She shook her head. "We're not. We're teachers in Korea, though."

"What is it like in Seoul? I hope that I can go someday."

"It's alright. Pretty hectic."

Jojo got excited. "I love Korea. Do you know Jeon Ji-hyeon? She is my favorite actor."

"No, I don't. I'm sorry," she said, her gaze fixed on the picture.

"Did you ever watch the drama *Jewel in the Palace*? 80% of Burmese people watched that drama."

"Why couldn't he have come in here and experienced this with me? Something's been wrong with him this whole trip."

Jojo wanted to continue talking about *Jewel in the Palace*, but said, "I don't know."

"He's drinking more, and he's acting really distant. I wish he would have not had so much beer at lunch and come in here with me."

"If I ever go somewhere with my wife, I will do everything with her."

"You're a better boyfriend than what I've got," the girlfriend said with a smile.

Jojo laughed. "Should we go back?"

"Sure," she answered. She let Jojo take the lead, and the two of them retraced their steps to the little opening whence they'd entered.

Leading the girlfriend back was easier than leading her to the statue, because she had clearly gained some familiarity with the inner labyrinth of the temple. Jojo gave her credit for being so adaptable, because she was better at picking up these subtleties than most of the tourists he had previously guided. She didn't make a sound when the bats fluttered past them, even if they flew right next to their faces. Jojo could sense a certain determination emanating from this particular tourist, and he guessed that she wanted to get out of the temple in order to gloat about the fact that she saw an ancient Buddha to her boyfriend.

After having been transported to what felt like another dimension, they reemerged into the world of rain, swaying trees, and disinterested boyfriends. The boyfriend sat on the wet ground, tossing and catching his girlfriend's helmet.

As the trio gathered themselves on the walkway, Jojo asked them if they wanted to come to his house and look at his sand paintings. This was the moment he had been waiting for; unlike other people he knew, Jojo liked to provide tourists with a memorable experience inside the temple with the headless Buddha before trying to unload his sand paintings on them. Judging from what they told him, some of his friends were extremely uncouth with their approach to peddling. Their method involved nothing outside of rushing up to the target and presenting their wares. No nuance, whatsoever.

The girlfriend was interested, and since the boyfriend was not in her good graces, he approved of her exploring her curiosity.

While walking over to the house, Jojo overheard the girlfriend say, "I was sick the whole time in Bangkok and didn't get to go out at all. Now we're here, with the opportunity to explore temples, and you don't do it with me? What is wrong with you?"

The boyfriend mumbled a response, but Jojo couldn't hear it over the rain. He led the couple into the little patio area of his home, told them to have a seat, and introduced them to his wife Chit. She didn't know English, so she merely nodded and smiled at the pair. She had spread a liberal amount of thanaka on her soft cheeks, as she did every day, because the yellow paste helped her keep a healthy complexion. After the introduction and stares from the foreigners, Jojo went into his sales pitch. His wife looked on.

He picked up the first painting from the top of the stack. It was on canvas fabric, with the painting being rough to the touch. The picture itself was a red elephant with green, yellow, and orange at play. Jojo showed the sand painting to them, and demonstrated that it was waterproof and could be stored in any fashion — crumbled up in a ball, even — but he noticed that he was not getting through to the couple. The girlfriend's tears streamed down her face, which was redder than Jojo had ever imagined a face could get. He stood there dumbfounded, with the crumpled elephant painting resting in his hand. Chit looked at him, shrugged her shoulders, and told him in Burmese that he still had to try to make the sale. He had gone through the trouble of taking the girlfriend into the temple to see the Buddha, and the whole reason behind it had been to warm her up to the idea of buying a sand painting or two. If she didn't buy anything now, it would have been a waste.

Jojo inched toward the seated couple and started, "You have a small backpack, so you can put thi—"

The boyfriend reached for his girlfriend's shoulder, but she peeled it off and smacked him in the face. Jojo checked to see if Khin had witnessed this. The boy was in the house, so he had not. The girlfriend crossed her arms and hunched over, averting her eyes from everyone in the vicinity. The chicken clucked. Jojo sat down and pulled another sand painting from the pile. This one was an elephant composed of seven women. He especially liked this one for its abstract nature.

As Jojo moved to present the painting to the couple, the girlfriend turned to the boyfriend, her wet ponytail smacking against her neck. She said, "Why would you ever fuck a Thai hooker while I was sick in the hotel bed? Are you nuts?!"

"I don't know. Curiosity, I guess?"

"That is literally the worst answer you could have given!" She smacked him across the face again. Now his face was as red as hers. "I thought you were ready to commit to this relationship, but that is clearly not the case if you are banging Thai hookers."

"It was only one."

Jojo looked over his shoulder at Chit, who flicked her wrist at him and goaded him on.

Jojo did his best to explain to her what was happening, but Chit told him that this was most likely going to be their only sales opportunity of the day. Jojo had no choice but to press on.

To the boyfriend, the girl said, "Fuck you, smart ass. You can stay here for the next couple of days like we planned, but I'm going back to Mandalay right now. Take me to the hotel."

"You know the flight is going to cost about 300 bucks, right?" The boyfriend said.

"I'd pay a thousand if it got me away from you."

"What about our extended layover in Bangkok before going back to Seoul?"

"I'll stay in Suvarnabhumi and wait by the gate. You can run back to your hooker."

Khin came outside and rushed to Chit's side. Jojo thought that it was fortunate that Khin hadn't started studying English yet.

Jojo also thought that he was not going to be making any kind of sale, so he withdrew the seven woman elephant painting. The couple scooped up their helmets and started off.

Before leaving the sitting area, however, the girlfriend said to Jojo, "Thanks for taking me into the temple."

This gave Jojo a start. He said, "You are welcome."

"How much for one of those sand paintings?"

Jojo said, "One for 15,000 kyats, two for 25,000."

The girlfriend grabbed the boyfriend's arms and said, "You're buying me the seven woman elephant painting. I need to at least get something out of this mess."

"But I won't have enough money for the rest of my time here."

"Boo hoo. Like fifteen bucks is going to make any difference. Buy me the fucking painting."

The boyfriend sighed and handed over three purple notes to Jojo, who in turn handed him the sand painting. He normally would have pressed the man to buy another, but he knew that this strategy wouldn't work on this occasion. After making sure all of their belongings had been gathered, the couple headed off.

Once they were out of eyesight, Chit sucked her teeth at Jojo. "You should have sold them one more," she said.

"I told you what was going on with them. That guy was a scumbag."

"Eh. She'll take him back."

"What makes you say that?"

"If she were totally done with him, she would not have asked him to buy her a painting. Why would she want a token to remember such a terrible day by?" Chit went back into the house. As she went in, Jojo sat down in his painting chair.

Jojo grabbed a canvas fabric that had a picture stenciled on it. It was a copy of one of the wall paintings in Ananda Temple. Jojo grabbed a brush, dipped it in the green watercolor, and painted. He stayed in the lines as much as possible. He wasn't perfect, but mistakes were easily corrected. Jojo went on like this the rest of the afternoon. Every once in a while, however, he glanced up, hoping that another foreign couple would pay him a visit.

North

For Jin-tae, June 25th, 1950 was not only the day the Korean War started, but it was the day his family was torn apart. His brother Gi-tae, a soldier for the North, was pressed into action on that summer morning and was never seen again. No matter how much time passed, the end of June was always the saddest time of the year for Jin-tae.

A couple of days after the sixty-sixth iteration of the day his brother disappeared, Jin-tae walked along the winding street to the fifty meter-wide channel to start his shift as a ferryman. He wore the same thing he did every day — jeans, a denim jacket over a t-shirt, and a newsboy cap. The denim had long ago been bleached by the salt in the air. Jin-tae operated the gaetbae, a small boat that worked by pulling on a cable that ran through wickets on each end of it. The gaetbae required at least one ferryman, usually two. Jin-tae held the post for years. After the bridge connecting both sides of the channel had been constructed, people only took the ferry for fun. It had become popular with tourists in recent years, partly because of its novelty but mostly because it had been featured in the drama *Autumn in My Heart*.

A waft of the familiar salty smell of the sea greeted him as he approached his workplace. It was the same olfactory sensation he'd felt when he came to the channel with Gi-tae as a child. The two of them used to love taking the gaetbae to the beach, where in the summer — under the watchful eye of the Japanese military police — they played by the sea.

Gi-tae had excelled at everything, especially skipping rocks. Jin-tae recalled the times his brother would sidearm stones that skipped a dozen times and traveled fifty meters, whereas he would take the same type of rock and have it plunk after one skip. When the tide was low, they'd scamper out into the intertidal zone and pluck whelks and abalone out of the sand. Gi-tae always managed to dig up more, with the writhing mollusks piled just below the top of his bucket.

Gi-tae was never boastful about his hauls, though. He was, after all, the one to teach Jin-tae how to cook the mollusks on the makeshift grill they had at home. The smoky flavor of the whelks always reminded Jin-tae of summer, and to this day he couldn't eat one without thinking of those carefree days spent with his brother.

The gaetbae lay idle in the narrow channel, the soft flow of the water lapping at its painted blue sides. This floating platform was one hundred percent utilitarian. It could fit a maximum of thirty people, and only traversed the narrow channel separating Abai Village on the east from Sokcho proper on the west. Jin-tae hopped on board, spryly for an octogenarian.

As he untied the gaetbae from the dock, he continued to think about his older brother, and the circumstances that led to him never being able to come home. Sokcho was located north of the 38th parallel, which meant that between the end of World War II and the end of the Korean War, it had been part of the North. During the war, Gi-tae had been taken prisoner by the South. When the fighting ended, and Sokcho had been ceded to the South, Gi-tae had been returned to the North.

Jin-tae now lived in a different country without ever leaving his hometown.

Around 1985, he heard that Gi-tae had settled in Wonsan, and this was the only information about his brother that he ever received. Jin-tae was never married, and since his parents were now passed, none of his acquaintances knew that he had a brother living north of the DMZ. In fact, the only living people he could think of who knew about his brother were those who'd rejected his requests every time the occasional round of family reunions came around.

When it was announced in 2015 that reunions would take place, and that lottery winners from all over the South would convene in Sokcho and take charter buses to meet their long-lost relatives just over the border at Mt. Kumgang Resort, Jin-tae applied as quickly as he could. The lottery, however, was fickle as always, and since only a few hundred of the tens of thousands of applicants were fortunate enough to take part in the reunions, Jin-tae was once again denied the chance to see Gi-tae. Because of his advanced age, he knew that this round of reunions had most likely been his last opportunity.

Ham Min-joon, Jin-tae's modern-day partner on the gaetbae, was late in arriving at the dock. He jogged as he approached, feigning embarrassment for being late. His job was to sit in the booth on the Abai Village side of the channel and collect passenger fares. Min-joon was much younger; Jin-tae supposed that he was in his early thirties. His enthusiasm made him wear a perpetual eye smile, with his tan, smooth skin bunching up in the corners, which led Jin-tae to believe that he would develop crow's feet as he aged. While the old man was disillusioned by the fact that the gaetbae, a centerpiece of his childhood with Gi-tae, had been transformed into somewhat of a tourist novelty, Mr. Ham reveled in it. He cared more about the unique experience the gaetbae offered tourists than he did the fact that it had persisted throughout Sokcho's tumultuous history, and Jin-tae did not approve of this stance.

One time, he'd boiled over because Min-joon had been ignorant of the fact that Sokcho had formerly been part of the North. Jin-tae took this ignorance as a slap in the face to all of those who had been separated from family members in the conflict, himself included. In fact, Abai Village was named in honor of those who could not return to their hometowns after the armistice. The village served as a sanctuary for Jin-tae and others in his position, and Min-joon had insulted them, which Jin-tae saw as egregious. How could any resident of Sokcho not know this vital information? Practically half the people in the city had relatives in the North. Jin-tae had been so enraged by Min-joon's lack of expertise on the subject that he needed to be restrained. Even after some half-hearted apologies, he hadn't fully forgiven Min-joon for this faux pas. These days, the two of them mostly talked about the weather when they saw each other.

"It's too cloudy today," Min-joon said as he hopped on the boat.

"Yeah. It is," Jin-tae responded.

"Do you think it will clear up later?"

"No."

"Really? It's the end of June. It should be sunny."

"Yeah, well, maybe it will be sunny tomorrow. Not today." Jin-tae ambled over to the rack on the side of the ferry and grabbed one of the metal rods hanging there.

Each rod had a hook at the end, not unlike a bent coat hanger. Jin-tae walked to the bow of the boat — if it could be called that — and hooked the rod to the iron cable that ran down the middle of the platform. He kept the rod hooked and walked back to the "stern," pulling while he walked. With that, the gaetbae gently inched toward the opposite dock. Min-joon stood and watched.

"Grab a rod," the old man grunted.

Min-joon rushed into service. He grabbed a rod, spun it until he had the grip he liked, and mirrored the process. Hook, pull, unhook, walk back to the bow, repeat. They repeated this manual process for five minutes until they reached the other side.

As they arrived in Abai Village, Min-joon disembarked and headed for his post. In that booth, under the overpass and the hum of passing traffic that came with it, Mr. Ham would be collecting two hundred won from every person who boarded the gaetbae that day. A week prior, Min-joon had bragged to Jin-tae that he knew two hundred won was about twenty US cents, which Jin-tae couldn't care less about. To him, two hundred won was simply two hundred won, and Min-joon cared too much about anything cosmopolitan. These thoughts remained in Jin-tae's mind as he regarded his coworker and repeated the process of traversing the channel, only back to the west dock. He was happy to be going it alone this time.

The first cluster of passengers awaited the gaetbae, eager to head over to Abai Village. Even before reaching his passengers, Jin-tae could hear Japanese being spoken. He knew the language from his early childhood, when it was the language of instruction at school. Sure enough, in among the crowd, there were three young Japanese women. One was tall and had bangs. Another was short, but had the same hairstyle and a mole on her cheek. The third was also short, but had long hair. All of them giggled with glee.

"I can't believe we're actually riding the boat from *Autumn in My Heart*," the tall one said, while all three of them reached for rods.

"That drama has to be the only reason anybody knows about this boat," the mole-specked one added. Jin-tae thought about the time in the early sixties when it was falsely reported that Gi-tae had returned, and he'd ferried over to Abai Village only to end up staring out at the sea. After they all had their rods, the long-haired one pulled her phone out of her bejeweled clutch and said, "Let's take a selfie." They set up accordingly, with the tall one holding the phone because her arm was longer.

"I'm Song Hye-gyo," the one with the mole said, holding the rod like a pitchfork to make sure it made it into the frame. She shifted her hips and tilted her head back, intently looking into the camera. Jin-tae watched the young women with disdain. Even he knew Song Hye-gyo was a famous actress, and that she was most certainly not this young woman.

The women took multiple shots, altering their poses each time. By the time they had taken a photo that met their approval, the boat was already halfway across the channel, having been pulled by Jin-tae and another passenger.

Once the phone was back in the clutch of the one with long hair, the group decided that it was time to address the task at hand. The one with the mole had a rough go at hooking the cable, prodding and smacking before finally latching it, only to have the rod slip off once she set to pulling. The other two cackled at this failure in dexterity, and decided that they would not be making fools of themselves on this day. They all hung the rods on the rack and remained near the railing.

Along with the rest of the passengers, the three women alighted and paid Min-joon, the coins clinking into the collection bucket. Jin-tae guessed that they would find other shooting locations from the show they enjoyed so much and take more pictures of themselves. Jin-tae wondered why everything in Sokcho had changed. Why didn't people come just to enjoy the food and the beach? Jin-tae couldn't think of any place in Korea that had better crab, and he saw that as enough of a reason to visit.

There still weren't many passengers departing Abai Village at this time of day, so the next load was paltry. As Jin-tae pulled the boat across the channel, he saw the squid boats docked just north of the gaetbae's designated path. Each one was outfitted with a couple dozen light bulbs fixed to poles outstretched port and starboard. These boats were always idly docked in the mornings, undulating in place. This was because squid fishing was done at night. The fishing crews took the vessels out into the East Sea in total darkness, and once they reached a shoal, they turned the lights on. Squid, because of their attraction to illumination, would head right into the trap. Squid was another type of seafood that Jin-tae thought was the best in all of Korea, and he loved all varieties — dried, grilled, or otherwise. His favorite squid dish was ojingeo sundae, which was Sokcho's take on blood sausage. The only similarity was the ingredients that were stuffed inside were. Thinking of ojingeo sundae made Jin-tae decide that he would head over to the market later and get some.

Jin-tae made a few more trips across the channel before deciding that he couldn't resist the urge for some ojingeo sundae. His arms were getting tired too, so he decided to finish his shift early. He'd long ago ceded managerial control to Min-joon and these days, he came and went as he pleased. Nobody ever expected him to work a full shift pulling the gaetbae, so he spent most of his time at the beach and market.

"Min-joon!" he barked at the toll booth. "Call the other guy and get him up here." Despite the "other guy" being a coworker of Jin-tae's, the old ferryman didn't know his name.

"Yes sir!" Min-joon obliged.

"I'll do one more round trip," he informed his colleague.

"Got it." Min-joon smiled at paying passengers as he pulled out his phone and called the "other guy." Without waiting to see whether his replacement was actually available to come on such short notice, Jin-tae embarked on the journey to the west dock.

By the time Jin-tae got to the western side of the channel, the replacement was already standing there. He had a restrained look on his face, and he tapped his foot anxiously. He did not make direct eye contact with Jin-tae, who simply greeted him and told him he would be finished after the next crossing. The replacement, who like everyone else was younger than Jin-tae, acknowledged him respectfully. He told his older colleague that he could relax on this crossing, and simply make sure that everyone stayed on board. Jin-tae sensed that the respect this ferryman paid him was fake, but he did not care; if he was over eighty years old and wanted to take the rest of the day off, he should be able to do so.

The last load of passengers lurched onto the gaetbae, and among them Jin-tae noticed a group of Westerners, which was admittedly a rare sight in Sokcho. They seemed to be holding themselves together well enough, except for one. This one glided on board with his eyes half open and a half finished bottle of grapefruit flavored soju in his hand. Jin-tae did not approve of people drinking on his boat, and thought that if this foreigner wanted to make a public embarrassment of himself like that, then he should have spent the weekend in Busan instead.

The young ferryman pulled on the cable and started the journey. Admittedly, Jin-tae thought his coworker had a certain knack worth admiring. Pulling the gaetbae wasn't particularly difficult for people once they understood the way it worked, but there wasn't anyone around who made pulling it look any easier than this guy did. Seeing him pull with such alacrity made the foreigners begin to chatter and take notice of the way the gaetbae was operated. Judging by the gestures they made, Jin-tae figured that they were talking about the rod and the cable.

After a good deal of hounding from the group, the one with the soju bottle emerged and moved to grab a rod, still with the bottle in hand. Jin-tae knew that this was not going to end well, so he tapped the young man on the arm and motioned for him to give the soju to one of his friends. The young man either did not understand or did not care. He shook Jin-tae off before hooking the rod onto the cable and pulling it with one hand while backpedaling to the stern. This tickled the rest of the foreigners in the group, who giggled and goaded him on. Jin-tae's colleague continued to work as briskly as ever, and the soju toter was successful in his first pull down the boat. He returned to the bow and hooked the cable one more time.

On his second go at pulling the gaetbae, the foreigner hammed it up much more than he had the first time, holding the bottle of soju in the air and attempting to drink from it as he pulled the cable. The liquor dribbled and splashed onto his face and shirt, and the group of friends erupted in raucous laughter.

Jin-tae marched up to the intoxicated tourist and tried to pull the rod from his hand. The young man resisted for a moment and glared at Jin-tae, but eventually relinquished the rod.

Jin-tae looked into the young man's dead eyes and said, in Korean, "You're embarrassing yourself. Do you have any idea what this boat is or what it represents?!" He turned and ferried the gaetbae across the channel.

The foreigner hadn't understood what Jin-tae said, and slurred a retort that Jin-tae felt wouldn't have been discernible even if it had been in Korean. After this brief exchange, the foreigner retreated to his group of friends, who laughed at Jin-tae while holding their hands to their mouths. Rather than escalate the situation, the old man simply kept his head down and continued his work.

The clouds broke, and the glass of the squid boat bulbs glimmered in the sunlight as the gaetbae reached the east dock. The passengers piled off, and as soon as he was off the boat, the drunken foreigner immediately started a commotion with Min-joon. Jin-tae's replacement left everyone behind, taking the next load of passengers across the channel. The foreigner and Min-joon went back and forth in English for a bit, and while Min-joon was able to speak the tourist's language, he clearly had a hard time articulating himself. He did his best to maintain his signature eye smile in the face of an anger he did not understand, but his patience didn't get through to the foreigner. Jin-tae backed away and observed the confrontation from a distance because he did not want anything more to do with this young man. The sun had just come out, and he wanted to put the day behind him. After one of the foreigner's friends tapped him on the shoulder and said something to him, he paid Min-joon two hundred won and skulked off into Abai Village.

Jin-tae walked up to Min-joon and asked, "What was he complaining about?"

Min-joon turned and snapped, "You! He was complaining about you and I had to answer for what you did."

"All I did was make sure everyone on the gaetbae was safe. And don't talk to me like that. I'm older than you are!"

"I'm sorry, but you know it's never good for us to have angry passengers."

"Was he still being a drunk idiot when you talked to him?"

"He said that you shoved him out of the way for no reason, and that because he only pulled the gaetbae for half of the channel, he wanted to pay half the price."

"That's ridiculous. He was drunk, and when he pulled the rod he looked like he was going to fall. He could have even gone overboard."

"Yeah well, you could have handled it a little bit more gently."

"What are you talking about?" Jin-tae took a step toward Min-joon.

"Do you think tourists will want to ride the gaetbae if the ferryman gets angry every time they do something wrong? It's a strange boat. Most people aren't going to know how to operate it the first time they ride it, and they don't need to be yelled at when they're unsure. They need to be guided."

"Nonsense," Jin-tae said as he flicked his wrist. "I'm going to the beach."

Min-joon looked at the ground and said, "Can you not come back for awhile?"

Jin-tae was flabbergasted. "How dare you! I've been doing this since before you could walk!"

Min-joon sighed. "I've been watching you for months, and I've tried to give you a chance, but you've become too abrasive for the tourists to enjoy their experience on the gaetbae. We'll call you when we need you."

Jin-tae stormed off. He felt Min-joon's eyes on his back and knew that that was the last of it. Once he was away from the dock, he walked into a convenience store and bought a bottle of makgeolli and paper cups to go along with it, forgetting all about the ojingeo sundae he'd been craving earlier. If he was going to relax at the beach, he might as well pair his views with some rice wine.

He found a bench at the beach and had himself a seat. Looking out at the sea always brought him to more peaceful center, because it brought him back to his time with Gi-tae. It was also helpful that he was in Abai Village, the only place in Sokcho that hadn't forgotten the past. The calming effect Abai Village had on this particular June 25th weekend caught Jin-tae by surprise, as he came to the realization that Min-joon or the tourists he ferried would never understand his perspective.

The sun had completely broken through the clouds and enveloped him with warmth. With the mountain and city behind him and the sea ahead, he watched the gulls squawk and bicker over a scrap of fried chicken. He took a sip of makgeolli and tasted a hint of paper along with the milky rice wine.

As the sea breeze swept gently across his face and the anger of the morning slid into his mind's recesses, Jin-tae decided that he was okay with giving up his work as a gaetbae operator.

As long as he could still come to Abai Village to look out at the East Sea and imagine that his brother was looking at that same calm blue expanse, he was fine.

Oyster Omelette

In a rush, Mei-ling cooked dinner for her family before she went to work. The potstickers crackled on the stove as she wheeled around to cut the guava slices that would serve as a sort of palate cleanser. She'd scoured her workplace for the perfect guavas, because her husband, Yu-hsuan, had scolded her for bringing home overripe fruit the week before. Somehow, even after combing through the market for the fruit, one of the bunch she eventually came home with was too soft. The soft one lay in her hand, asking to be eaten before it turned.

Mei-ling worked at Shilin Night Market, which was the largest of its kind in Taipei. It was exhausting work most nights. Remembering the way her husband felt about soft guava, she set the bad one aside so that she could throw it in the trash later. The way it always went — and the way it would go if she were to feed him this old guava — consisted of him pointing his finger in her face and telling her that eating bruised guavas was the same as eating food scraps, and that that was what livestock ate. They were not a family of livestock.

The knife slid crisply through a fresh guava, with a gentle mist emanating from the incision. Mei-ling thought about the amount of time she'd spent rubbing her hands over the leathery fruits to discern their ripeness, despite the judging eyes of the proprietors. They didn't like when people lingered at their stalls for too long. Once she'd found the perfect guava or two, she had to engage in a haggling war with the stall owner, eventually relenting on a middle ground that was not-so-middle. It went on like this at each stall that she visited, because Yu-hsuan would only be satisfied if she brought home four perfectly ripe guavas. She knew most of these proprietors, but this recent pattern of searching the entire market for the perfect fruit was causing her reputation to wither, and she knew it. Mei-ling sympathized, however. She'd tire of her herself too if she spent an inordinate amount of time at her stall without spending much money. Maybe the thought of her dwindling reputation was what led to her slipping up and buying a soft guava. Maybe it was something else.

Thinking about it all caused her to lose her concentration, and the rate at which she cut the guava accelerated. As the anger inside her rose to a crescendo, the knife came down on her left index finger, slicing it open. Mei-ling cried out as she put the finger in her mouth to suck away the blood. It tasted metallic, like the time she held extra nails in her mouth while her dad hammered up the bookshelf in her room. She pulled her finger out of her mouth and assessed the damage. The cut was shallow and about one-and-a-half centimeters long, which was much milder than she'd initially expected. When she removed her mouth from the cut, blood pooled on the tip of her finger. The knife, with a smudge of blood remaining on its edge, lay passively next to the half-cut guava as Mei-ling shuffled to the bathroom to dress the wound.

When Mei-ling finished preparing dinner, she went into the bedroom to tell Yu-hsuan that it was ready. He lay on the bed with the TV on, watching baseball. The Lamigo Monkeys, his favorite team, were doing battle with the Chinatrust Brothers, and it was the first inning.

"Dinner is ready, darling," she said with a smile.

He said nothing as the light from the TV reflecting off of his glasses.

"Honey," she said.

"What?" he snapped, keeping his eyes on the game.

"Come get your dinner."

"I heard you the first time."

"Okay, just make sure you come out here before it gets cold."

"I know how to eat my dinner, Mei-ling."

Knowing that she had done all that she could to get Yu-hsuan to come out and eat, Mei-ling walked through their two-bedroom apartment to her son Chih-wei's room.

"Sweetheart, it's time to eat," she called out while slipping past the metal drying rack set up in the living room.

She was met with silence.

"Chih-wei?"

She gently pushed the door open, eliciting a soft groan from the hinges. Her eight-year-old son was also engaged in the same way that his father was, although he was playing a game on the computer instead of watching baseball. His ears were fully encased by his headphones, the most expensive pair that had been available the day she bought them in the mall. He'd threatened her with a tantrum if she didn't get them for him. She relented.

Mei-ling waved her hand softly, so as to not come off as demanding. "Sweetheart."

He glared at her and ripped the headphones off his ears. "I'm playing *League of Legends*, Mom!" He put his headphones on.

"I know, but you have to eat your dinner. I made pot-stickers and sliced some guava."

"I'm trying to bait some asshole so that I can get an ace, and if I stop right now, it'll ruin everything."

She didn't know what any of that meant, but she knew that she heard a bad word in there. "No bad words, Chih-wei."

He slammed his headset on the desk. "You just distracted me, and now I'm dead. You ruin everything!" He walked up to her and slapped her arm.

"Don't hit your mom," she said.

"Why not!" he shouted, slapping her again.

"How about I bring your dinner in here for you? That way you can keep playing while you eat." If she was being perfectly honest with herself, she was afraid of her son.

He nodded, put on his headphones, and resumed his game.

She went back out to the living room and toward the kitchen, sliding her socked feet on the papered floor. The food on the table wasn't nearly as plentiful as it had been when she'd gone to tell her son that dinner was ready. She immediately ascertained that her husband had come out of the bedroom, collected his food, and returned to the room to watch the game while he ate. These suspicions were confirmed when Yu-hsuan shouted from the bedroom that the potstickers were cold. Mei-ling prepared a plate for her son and brought it to his room, careful not to disturb him in the middle of his game. He grunted with approval when she set the food down on his desk.

Mei-ling sat eating her dinner alone at the kitchen table. Yu-hsuan could have been wrong about the potstickers before, but he was right now. They were cold. She ate them slowly and stared off into the distance, wondering what she could do to get her family to eat together and enjoy each other's company again. She didn't remember the last time they'd had a dinner like that. Maybe it was back when Chih-wei was a baby, but even those memories were polluted by Yu-hsuan's frustration with the baby's inability to keep the mushy food in his mouth.

Mei-ling remembered that her family always ate together when she was young, and some of her best memories came from dinners. Her current solitude made the room faround her feel colder than the potstickers.

She got a text message from her friend saying that she wouldn't be able to make it to work that night because her baby was sick. Mei-ling felt a cold potsticker slide down her throat as it dawned on her that she'd be alone at work, too. She ate about half of the potstickers and none of the guava, and mindlessly cleaned up and did the dishes before leaving for work. She was sure to say goodbye to her family before she headed out, but the biggest reaction she got was a subtle flick of the wrist from Yu-hsuan. While putting her shoes on, she grabbed her red fanny pack out of the closet next to the door. It was the same one she kept her money in while she worked throughout her entire career. When she strapped it on, she realized that Yu-hsuan probably didn't know it existed. He never saw her off, so there was no reason for him to ever have seen it.

Jiantan Station was thronged with people when Mei-ling worked her way down the stairs.

Typhoon Dujuan had struck two weeks earlier, but Taipei had recovered quickly and public transportation was crowded again. Nearly everyone in the station was on their way to Shilin. The place was a monstrous, multilevel complex with nearly every kind of Taiwanese cuisine and souvenir that one could imagine. Mei-ling had worked at the market since she was young, and after her parents were killed by Typhoon Nari in September 2001, she took over the family stall. She'd already been married to Yu-hsuan and questioned whether keeping the stall open was the right decision, but ultimately decided that her parents would want her to keep the family business going. She and Yu-hsuan tried for five years to start their own family, and were eventually granted with Chih-wei.

Mei-ling didn't own a fruit stand like the other stalls that she frequented for the sake of perfect guava, but a game stall. In years past, they had customers throw darts at balloons in order to win prizes, but she'd realized that this was costing them money. The game was far too easy, and customers were popping nearly every balloon and winning all of the biggest prizes. In order to fix this problem, Mei-ling decided to change the format of the game. Instead of darts, customers now had to pop balloons with a bow and arrow. She fashioned three styrofoam boards into balloon holders, with holes that accommodated balloons of different sizes. Different sizes of targets corresponded with different point values. Most contestants tried to hit the smaller, more valuable targets in a show of hubris. The styrofoam boards corresponded with three sets of bows and arrows that she had placed in front of a counter three meters away. This gaming format proved to be much more difficult than throwing darts at balloons, and funner, too. The biggest benefit was that it resulted in her not needing to buy as many stuffed Winnie the Poohs, SpongeBobs, or Totoros. Mei-ling thought that her parents would have been proud of her for making the change and improving the stall.

No matter how many times she went to the market, she was always taken in by the sights and smells. Lights of all colors illuminated the crowded path and beckoned visitors to come spend their money on clothes, food, and souvenirs. Stinky tofu dominated the scent profile one moment, while savory chicken skewers overpowered the next. For as taxing as the work was, Mei-ling was thankful to be working in such a lively environment. Setting the booth up had become routine for her by this point, and as a result she took all of the balloons she needed out of the locked compartment beneath the prizes and blew them up with her electric pump without even focusing on the task. The same routine applied to the bows and arrows. She'd kept the same bows for years, and only needed to tighten and replace the strings occasionally. The taxing part of the job was handling all of the transactions with customers and making sure that they didn't cheat by attempting to shoot more arrows than they had bought.

The early portion of the market's operating hours consisted mostly of older people buying their groceries. This was the exact reason why Mei-ling didn't arrive before the official opening of the market at 3 P.M., but later on. There was no need for her to stand around and expect grandmothers to shoot an arrow at balloons. She knew that the pace would pick up, however, so she wasn't worried about the slow start to the evening. If anything, a lack of customers early on might help her conserve energy for the rush.

She watched passersby. Many of their faces flushed a light red because of the Taiwan Beer they had most likely been drinking as a complement to their beef lamian or oyster omelettes. While it usually didn't bother her, the thought of these strangers' enjoyment nagged at her on this particular night. Once she thought about them eating oyster omelettes, she couldn't help but remember the first time she ever tried one. It had been when she was about six or seven years old and her mom had made them in their kitchen. Mei-ling still remembered the plant that sat in the windowsill above the sink, bathing in the sunlight. It was a pachira, otherwise known as a money tree. She didn't think that its small size was a coincidence. One particular evening, with everyone present, her mom plopped a plate of what looked like eggs covered in vomit onto the table. Mei-ling was hesitant to eat the dish at first, citing the disgusting appearance, but her mother urged her on. When she continued to hesitate, her father intervened.

"If you eat the oyster omelette, you will become a strong girl."

"Really?"

"Yes. If you eat a lot of them, you will grow fifty centimeters and be able to beat up all of the boys at school."

She smiled and dug her cheek into her collarbone.

"Sounds good, doesn't it?"

She nodded excitedly.

Her father chuckled. "Make sure you eat it before it gets cold. Otherwise, you won't grow as quickly."

Mei-ling never grew quickly enough to beat up all of the boys at school, but oyster omelettes became her favorite food. Yu-hsuan and Chih-wei, however, were never able to get past the unsightly appearance, so she hadn't eaten one in a long time.

Soon enough, the passing crowd drew their attention to her stall. Most of the contestants were young men attempting to win stuffed animals for their girlfriends, many of whom were preoccupied with taking selfies of themselves as their boyfriends took aim in the background.

Mei-ling surmised that they would be sharing the pictures on LINE with captions describing how manly their men were. Most likely, they would leave out the part where the boy missed all of the balloons and Mei-ling took his money.

There was a regular Robin Hood in the bunch every once in awhile, but most people didn't even know how to hold a bow correctly. Mei-ling herself never received any formal training in archery, and only learned by watching the form that winning customers used. If anyone was particularly hopeless, she'd help them by urging them to keep their elbow up and telling them how to properly nock the arrow, only because she knew that they would still miss and that her kindness would lead to them spending more money on a second bundle of arrows. It was better to have customers nearly miss than be entirely inept, because that shred of hope is what led to more attempts, and thus additional earnings.

All of the interactions played out as usual. It took a few minutes to adjust to her hand being bandaged, but Mei-ling established a rhythm to the way in which she handled the transactions. She wore the red fanny pack when she worked, and kept all of her money arranged in a particular way — big bills nearest — so that she could operate with greater efficiency. On this night, the rhythm was especially necessary because of the fact that she was working alone.

A young teenage couple approached the booth. The girlfriend was pretty — she had high cheekbones, large eyes, and a contoured chin. She actually looked like Mei-ling, before the typhoon and stress of raising a son hit her. Another difference was that this girl was going for a cute aesthetic, which Mei-ling had never done. She wore overall denim shorts over a white t-shirt. What really stood out about her look, however, was that she had a sprout coming out of her head. It wasn't real, but a hairpin with a rubber sprout attached. The extension swayed gently with any movement the girl made, but danced when she bounced with glee at the sight of the balloon shooting stall. Her boyfriend was skinny, had acne, and wore all black clothing. Something about him reminded Mei-ling of her own son. It might have been the fact that he stood with crossed arms and knitted brows as he watched the activity of the game stall. Mei-ling imagined that this boy also played *League of Legends*, that game that consumed so much of Chih-wei's time.

Despite the excitement that the sprout girl showed when other people shot arrows at balloons, the couple didn't make any moves to play the game. Instead, they stood in front of the stall watching. This went on for a few moments, and Mei-ling noticed out of the corner of her eye as she tended to customers down the line. She noticed that when interested customers approached the stall, they were repelled by the sprout girl cheering excitedly. Some of them ducked out of the way of the swaying sprout, as if they thought it was going to smack them in the face. The girl was completely unaware of those around her. This threw off the rhythm of the game, but Mei-ling waited patiently.

"I want to play," the girl said, clapping her hands.

"It looks stupid," the boy replied as he attempted to grab her hand.

"Come on, just let me do it," the sprout girl said.

The boy walked away without saying a word. It took a moment for the sprout girl to notice, but she followed once she did.

Mei-ling felt a sense of dread creep into her as subtly as the changing of the tides. In between handling cash, replacing balloons, and handing out prizes, she rubbed her hands together nervously, careful to avoid touching her wounded finger.

She was too busy with the business of the game stall to immediately notice the foreign couple that approached. Foreigners were fairly common at Shilin Night Market, as it was frequently listed on travel websites as one of the main attractions of Taipei. Mei-ling had taken it upon herself to learn basic English in order to communicate with international visitors. It had been more difficult than she anticipated, but she was better than most people around her now.

"Hey check this out," a male voice cut through the crowd.

"What is it?" a female voice replied.

Mei-ling looked at the duo. She didn't think that they were dating, because they were standing apart rather than holding hands. They didn't exude affectionate qualities. The young man had brown hair, and the young woman's hair was curly and black. Mei-ling also had black hair, but she found the young woman's curls to be fascinating. They wound loosely down past her shoulders, forming a bunch of helices reminiscent of the DNA models she used to see in school. The boyfriend wasn't attractive, in her opinion. He had a double chin and his face was pink, but it didn't look like it was that way because of drinking beer. It was natural, and Mei-ling didn't like it.

"Hello," she greeted them with a smile.

"What game?" the boyfriend said, gesturing demonstratively.

"You shoot the arrow and pop the balloon," Mei-ling said. Many customers, despite the self-explanatory setup of her booth, didn't know what the game was until she told them.

"Wow, your English is so good," the young man said. The young woman subtly shook her head.

Mei-ling smiled and said, "Five arrows for three hundred, ten for five hundred."

The young woman pulled three one-hundred New Taiwan dollar bills out of her black pleather purse and handed them to Mei-ling. "I'll have five arrows, please."

Mei-ling took the bills with her good hand, retrieved the arrows, and handed them to the young woman, who struggled to nock the first arrow. Every time she brought it up, she was unable to keep it aligned over her leading index finger, and it would slip out of her grip.

"Can I do it?" the young man said.

The girl rolled her eyes, but the boy couldn't see that.

When she turned around to hand him the bow, he pulled his chin back and made a double chin.

"Is that supposed to be funny?" She said.

The boyfriend giggled nervously and said, "I thought you might like it."

"Well I don't. You look gross," the young woman said as she handed him the bow.

The young man relaxed his neck and took the bow. After he missed his first shot, the young woman yanked the bow out of his hands, which shocked him. It shocked Mei-ling, as well. "I'm so sick of you trying to be funny," the young woman said, pulling the bow up. This time, she had no problem taking aim. When she shot, she missed the balloon, but the arrow dug into the styrofoam board with an authoritative thud. She reloaded, and without looking at the young man, she added, "Being gross isn't funny."

The young man wore a confused smile and said, "Can you just drop it?" He tried to put his hand on his companion's shoulder. She shrugged him off and shot the arrow. This time she not only popped a balloon, but it was one of the small ones. On her third shot, she popped another one of the smaller balloons. Murmurs grew among the surrounding crowd.

Since all of the small balloons had been eradicated from that particular board, Mei-ling had to put a hold on the young woman's round of shooting in order to fill the small holes with the appropriate targets.

As she bent down to grab the right balloons, she over-heard the young woman say, "This was a mistake." Mei-ling didn't think that the young woman could have been referring to the arrows that she had shot, because she had been near-perfect in that regard.

The moment Mei-ling put balloons into the open cutouts and got out of the way, the young woman popped one of them with her last arrow. The crowd cheered. Some among them had been filming the whole thing on their phones, impressed with the tourist's archery skills. Despite putting on an impressive show and being the center of spontaneous fanfare, the young woman did not smile.

All she said was, "I guess beer makes me good at archery."

"Which one do you want?" Mei-ling asked, gesturing to the stuffed animals on the shelf behind her.

"Take the giant Stitch," the young man said, pointing at the dog-like Disney creature.

"Fuck off," the young woman replied, rolling her eyes.

Mei-ling was amazed that this woman would speak to her boyfriend in such a way. She must have gasped audibly, because the young woman turned her attention to her.

"Give me the SpongeBob, please," she said.

"Yes," Mei-ling replied, the corners of her mouth fixed to her cheeks. She pulled out the ladder, leaned it on the shelf, climbed up, and retrieved the prize.

After the young woman was in possession of the Krusty Krab's fry cook, her companion reached out to grab him. It was clear that he wanted to at least appear to be gentlemanly by carrying the prize, but the young woman pulled away from him and indicated that she would be holding SpongeBob. The young man reached his right hand into his pocket.

"I'll have ten arrows, please," he said, pulling out a one hundred New Taiwan dollar bill. "It's five hundred," Mei-ling replied, holding up five fingers.

"No, ten."

"Ten arrows, five hundred New Taiwan dollars."

The young man smiled nervously and pulled the bill closer to his face to inspect it.

The young woman laughed, removing one of the hands supporting SpongeBob to cover her mouth.

The boyfriend proved to less accurate than his companion. He managed to hit the first balloon, a large one at the center of the board, and this managed to keep the surrounding crowd engaged for a moment, but he promptly missed the rest of his shots. As he progressed through his shots, his shoulders grew increasingly stooped, and his aim was increasingly limp. By the end of his round, nobody was watching.

"Looks like I don't have it," the young man said to his partner when he was finished. The only problem was that she had already walked away. It was another action that surprised Mei-ling. Yu-hsuan would never put up with her doing the same thing.

Mei-ling felt that she was able to successfully manage the stall, and that she deserved to finish work early that night. She thought she'd made enough money for being by herself and having a bad finger, so she announced to the crowd that she would be closing the stall early. The news was met with little more than grumbles.

Now that Mei-ling had a couple extra hours, she didn't know what to do with them. After the smells of the market hit her nostrils, however, she knew where she would go.

The basement level of Shilin Night Market was completely different from the upstairs portion of the place. The yellow tables, with their color made more vibrant by the fluorescent lights hung above them, littered the space and created a cramped atmosphere. Chinese signage hung from the ceiling in nearly every place that it could, with each placard written in different colors in order to stick out. Most stalls were situated in the middle of the room, but the proprietors of wall stalls chose to decorate their areas with clocks, calendars, and personal effects so heavily that the peeling wallpaper was barely visible. Whereas the food stalls upstairs primarily sold fruit, with the occasional skewer or stinky tofu stall peppering the outer boundaries of the market, every stall in the basement was filled with employees cooking up Taiwanese fare. None of the many aromas floating throughout the room distracted Mei-ling from what she came for. She went straight to the oyster omelette stall.

The hawker at the stall seemed to know what she was doing. Her brow was furrowed at all times — it did not matter whether she was making food, handling money, or serving the customers seated at the tables directly in front of the stall. She wore a white bandana and yellow apron that matched the table tops. Mei-ling ordered an oyster omelette and a bottle of Taiwan Beer. The bottles were big enough for three or four glasses, but she didn't mind. She'd drink it all by herself if she had to. Before Mei-ling was able to say "please," the woman told her to pay one-hundred fifty New Taiwan dollars.

Mei-ling sat and waited for the order to come out. She decided to face the crowd in her seat, so that she could people-watch. Even though she worked at Shilin, she was never able to focus on the crowd without having to worry about her business. Without any responsibilities, she was able to see the couples laughing and smiling as they walked past arm in arm. She could not remember laughing as genuinely as they did. She also saw a mother leading her daughter, a pigtailed girl clad in pink from head to toe who happily held her mother's hand in one hand and a star fruit in the other.

Chih-wei always groaned — and screamed, if bored enough — whenever she brought him to the market.

While she was watching the crowd, Mei-ling noticed a familiar head of black hair. It was the Katniss Everdeen from earlier. She approached the oyster omelette stall without feeling Mei-ling's eyes. The young woman looked at the hanging menu like she was trying to decode the Enigma machine.

"Hey, over here!" Mei-ling said in English, hoping that she was loud and clear enough to get the woman's attention.

To Mei-ling's surprise, the young woman heard her and looked over.

"Hi! You shoot arrows well!" Mei-ling said, unsure of how exactly she should start the conversation.

This worked, though. The tourist smiled and approached Mei-ling. "Are you the woman from the bow and arrow stall?"

"Yes, I am. Have a seat." Mei-ling pushed the metal chair opposite her out with her toes.

It screeched on the floor.

"Sure, why not," the tourist said as she sat down. "I really like your booth. I've never seen anything like it before."

"You're really good at shooting arrows," Mei-ling said. She had been unsure of what Katniss said, so she tried to cover up that fact by repeating herself.

"Thanks. Just got lucky, I s'pose."

"First time in Taipei?"

"It is."

"What do you think?"

"I love it. I wish other places had night markets like this."

The woman who took Mei-ling's order placed her oyster omelette and beer on the table.

A napkin and set of disposable wooden chopsticks followed. Everything clacked as it was set down.

"Is this an oyster omelette?" the tourist asked.

"Yes. You want some?"

"No. I'm a vegetarian."

"Vegetarian?"

"Yeah. I don't eat any meat."

"Really?"

"Yes. No meat."

"That's too bad."

The foreigner shrugged her shoulders and gestured at the omelette. "Is it any good?"

"It's my favorite."

The young woman stared at it uneasily.

"I know. It looks terrible, but the taste is great."

"Fine. I'm not in Taiwan often, so I might as well cheat."

Mei-ling smiled and asked the hawker for an extra plate, beer glass, and set of chopsticks.

Once everything was in place, Mei-ling sawed off a piece of the omelette and placed it on her companion's plate, sure to include an oyster and a bit of the sauce in the bite.

As soon as she had the morsel in her mouth, the young woman's eyes bulged in amazement. "Oh my god," she said with her hand over her mouth, her words muffled by the omelette. "This is so good."

Mei-ling laughed. "The best."

The young woman thought as she ate, and said, "I guess I shouldn't judge a book by its cover."

"What about books?"

"It's an English expression. It means that I shouldn't think something is bad because it looks bad."

Mei-ling nodded and said, "Or that something is good because it looks good."

"Yeah that too."

Mei-ling smiled as she chewed her omelette. The sauce was better than she remembered. The miso paste, when done right, made the flavor transcendent. This miso sauce was done right. She set her chopsticks down and took a swig of beer.

"My name is Charlotte," the young woman said, extending her hand across the table. "What's your name?"

Mei-ling paused her eating to say her name and shake Charlotte's hand.

"That's such a pretty name," Charlotte said. "Let's get another omelette."

Mei-ling laughed and handled the order in Mandarin.

The two women devoured their second omelette and ended up ordering a third. They enjoyed each other's company in the basement level of the Shilin Night Market. To Mei-ling, there was nothing better than oyster omelettes, beer, and good company. Before they parted ways, Mei-ling haggled her way into buying some of the ingredients, mostly by assuring the hawker that Charlotte was going to sing the praises of the stall on her blog, thus garnering some international recognition. When they finished their food, they thanked each other, promised to connect with each other on Facebook, and parted ways, never to meet again.

The next morning, Mei-ling was expected to prepare breakfast for Yu-hsuan and Chih-wei. The night before, of course, she'd forwent her evening routine of buying new guava in order to spend time with Charlotte. She did not care whether Yu-hsuan would get upset about the lack of new guava. On the other hand, Mei-ling suspected that there was a chance that he wouldn't even notice. Another part of her routine that she ignored in favor of hanging out with Charlotte was preparing the dough for the youtiao that Yu-hsuan and Chih-wei would eat for breakfast. Her husband expected her to do this every night, even after times she closed the game stall around 1 a.m. Her husband viewed the fried pastry as an absolute must for breakfast, and did not care that she finished work so late — it was not going to stop him from eating his favorite breakfast food. This omission would certainly be noticed. The only part of her routine that she did follow was putting her red fanny pack in the closet next to the front door when she arrived.

Not only was the breakfast devoid of fresh guava and youtiao, it was missing all of the other trappings of a typical breakfast in the household. Instead, Mei-ling made oyster om-elettes. She wanted to see if she could share the experience of the night before, and was steadfast in her mindset that this was going to be an enjoyable breakfast. She thought that her family shouldn't think bad covers made bad books, or however the expression went.

Rousing Yu-hsuan and Chih-wei into the kitchen took the usual convincing on Mei-ling's part, with both of them complaining that her presence was annoying. They happened to come out of their rooms at the same time.

"What the hell is this?" Yu-hsuan said as he stroked his matted hair.

"Where is my youtiao?!" Chih-wei screamed at a decibel level far too high for the time of day. The neighbors most likely heard it, but they were probably used to that tone by now.

Mei-ling took a deep breath to compose herself. "Today we are going to eat oyster omelettes," she said, struggling to keep her hands steady. "It's my favorite food, and I want you to try it, my Chih-wei." She sat down, cut off a big piece, and put it in her mouth. "Mmm, this is really good!" she said. "It's really yummy, and it will make you stronger than all of the kids at school," she added.

"I'm already stronger than all of the kids at school," Chih-wei said, rolling his eyes. "Oysters are gross."

"I don't like it," Yu-hsuan added. "You should have asked me if this was okay before you went and made such a disgusting dish."

"And that's why I didn't tell you anything!" Mei-ling snapped. "If you never open yourself up to anything new, you will never know what is best!"

Yu-hsuan wrinkled his brow. "What's that supposed to mean? Are you sleeping with someone?"

"No. All I want is for us to try new food."

"Mom is cheating on Dad!"

Mei-ling said, "Do my wants not matter?"

Yu-hsuan scoffed. "Shut up. You don't know what you're talking about."

Chih-wei shouted, "Shut up, Mom! You stupid bitch!"

He took a hard swing at her stomach, but rather than let it land, Mei-ling grabbed his wrist. He yelped at a new decibel level. "Listen here, you little brat. If your mom wants you to try something new, you try something new." She'd never felt so alive.

"Let go of my son!" Yu-hsuan shouted. He pried at Mei-ling's hand and said, "It's okay, Chih-wei. The bad lady won't hurt you."

"Bad lady?!" Mei-ling shrieked as she released Chih-wei's arm with a twist, causing him to yelp even louder as he crumpled to the floor. Yu-hsuan tended to the boy on the ground. The image made Mei-ling furious.

She walked over to where she placed the old guava on the counter the night before and grabbed the mushy fruit. In one motion, she pulled a knife from the woodblock and sliced the skin off of the fruit. She was too enraged to note how impressive it was for her to do so with a bandaged hand. She put the knife down and walked over to the kitchen table while her husband was still kneeling on the floor with their son. She took the fruit, which was bordering on rotten, and smashed it onto the table.

"Eat it," she said.

"I'm not going to eat that," Yu-hsuan said. "It's rotten."

"Either eat that or the oyster omelette."

Chi-wei whimpered.

Mei-ling looked at him and said, "Shut up and eat your food. Both of you."

They hesitated, and Mei-ling grabbed the plates. "Fine," she said. "I'll eat them all myself."

She took the plates into the bedroom and kicked the door shut. By the time she finished the oyster omelettes and came out of the bedroom, the kitchen was empty. But the guava had been cleaned off the table.

Customer Service

Working at the United Airlines Customer Service Desk at O'Hare wasn't the best job in the world, but Glen thought it was. Some of the tasks he had to perform on a daily basis were too unsavory for most people, but not for Glen. Whenever he negotiated a rent extension with his landlord, he wasn't able to push the deadline back in any substantial way, but he nearly always got his way when he dealt with customers at the airport. He sat as upright as stop sign in a rich neighborhood, and kept his nametag perfectly perpendicular to his frame. A walkie talkie was clipped to his navy blue sweater vest, and added to his air of authority. He had thin hair the color of a field mouse, and kept it combed forward in order to conceal the bald spot on the top of his head that he didn't want to acknowledge existed.

On one particular night, Flight 1747 to Tokyo Narita, had been delayed, and Glen was excited to squash the dreams of souls unfortunate enough to think he would help them. The official word was that the flight had been delayed four hours due to "maintenance issues," but everyone who worked for the airline knew that was code for, "There was a mistake in routing, and the plane is not actually here. When pressed for details, make up whatever you want."

After shuffling someone off with more questions than when they had first approached him, Glen looked at the passengers in the sparse line and waved the next one over. It was an obese woman in her mid-twenties, and Glen wasn't happy. He didn't respect overweight women because he did not find them to be sexually attractive, and he considered speaking with them to be a waste of time. His reasoning was that if there was no possibility of a sexual encounter with a woman, then there was no need for interaction. The same prejudice applied to women with any other physical characteristic Glen deemed to be a deformity — including, but not limited to, missing teeth, burns, unsightly birthmarks, and freckles.

The woman didn't notice the first two waves that Glen gave her, and she only came over after he called out to her. He grew incensed at the sight of her, and tears of anger welled up in his eyes.

Once Glen blinked away the tears, he saw that the woman standing before him was clearly stoned. Her eyes wandered, and a nervous smirk sat on her face as she sniffled.

Considering the fact that she was odorless, Glen guessed that instead of smoking a joint, she had eaten edibles before going through security.

"Hello, ma'am. How can I help you?" Glen said.

"Yeah, um, can you tell me where my flight is?" Her eyes were crimson, and she was unsure of where to set her carry-on bag. There was a minor fray on the corner of the bag, and Glen assumed that it was due to the woman not knowing how to take care of her belongings.

"Sure. May I see your boarding pass, please?"

"Yeah. Let me get it real quick," she said as she dug around in her purse. After scraping around for a bit, she fished out her boarding pass and handed it to Glen.

Glen noticed that the woman's fingertips, clearly stained by Flamin' Hot Cheetos, were as red as her eyes. The boarding pass was also stained by the dust. Glen flipped it over, saw what it really was, and said, "Ma'am, this is a receipt."

"What?"

"This isn't a boarding pass. It's a receipt for . . ." Glen paused to read the stained slip of paper. "Cinnabon. You didn't eat your boarding pass, did you?"

"What?" the woman giggled nervously.

"I asked if maybe you misplaced your boarding pass," Glen said.

"Oh," she said as she dug around in her purse again and came up with the boarding pass.

It was authentic this time.

Glen read the ticket and said, "The gate for your flight to Denver is twenty feet to my left. It's boarding now, so you should hurry." He handed the boarding pass back to the woman.

She snorted and said, "Thank you."

Seeing a window before she had a chance to wheel away her carry-on bag, Glen said, "Just a moment, ma'am. It appears that your carry-on is not up to code. I'm going to have to charge you twenty-five dollars."

"What?"

"Your bag. It's — That fray in the corner makes it a safety risk. The contents of your bag could spill out, and there is no telling what kind of reaction that could cause with other passengers, or even with other bags if we were to decide to check it and put it underneath. Now I could allow you to bring it onboard, but I have to charge you a nominal fee. Either that, or we can take it to the incinerator."

"I've never heard of that rule before," the woman murmured.

"It's a new policy," Glen said, his confidence growing. "I'm going to have to ask that you pay twenty-five dollars. And since we're still working this rule in, I can only take cash."

"That's not real," the woman said. "Can I speak to your manager?"

"I'm sorry ma'am, but I am the manager," Glen said, shocked that the woman had somehow mustered up the audacity to defy him. "Even if you try to go over my head, who is the airline going to believe: me, or the stoned customer who can't stand up straight? I could report you to the TSA for being under the influence of marijuana, and they could have you barred from the flight."

The woman sighed and reached back into her purse. She was unwilling to risk missing her flight over Glen's contrived baggage regulation.

"That's right," Glen said, his palm facing upward. "Fork it over." He printed out a blank boarding pass and told her it was a receipt. "I bet you can't wait to get to Denver, Cheech."

She gave him the money and stumbled away.

"Enjoy your flight, ma'am," Glen said, loud enough so that the other customers could hear him. He glanced at Scott, his coworker seated to his left, and smirked before pocketing the money. Scott —whose spiked hair looked perpetually wet — returned a knowing glance and continued his interaction with a confused middle-aged couple. Seated next to Scott was Teresa, who was too busy dealing with an old woman demanding an upgrade to notice what Glen had done. Glen hated Teresa, outwardly because she was too nice to the customers, and inwardly because she wasn't attracted to him.

Glen waved the next passenger to the desk and started to prepare himself for how he could shatter this one's dreams. He was feeling good about having just earned a little extra cash, and he wanted to ride that high into the next customer interaction.

This passenger was a man in his twenties, and he looked angry. Glen dealt with plenty of angry people in his line of work, so this was not something that threw him off his game. If anything, he relished passenger anger. It allowed him more leeway in the improvisations he could make. If he said something particularly offensive and the passenger complained, he could either point to the passenger misremembering in their emotional state or his being provoked by the customer's rudeness. The young man gripped the counter so tightly that his fingertips expanded. He had a cobalt ring on his index finger.

"How may I help you, sir?" Glen said. He looked up at the customer and saw exasperation.

"I'm supposed to be on the flight to Narita, which got delayed and moved to a new gate.

The employees at the first gate told all of us that we could rebook our connections at the new gate, but —"

"That's correct," Glen said, the interruption intentional. "You have to rebook at the gate, not the Customer Service desk."

"But there's nobody at the gate."

"There will be shortly. Now if you will, sir, could you please allow me to deal with passengers on other flights?" Glen waved up the next passenger.

The young man took a deep breath. He composed himself and said, "I need to get to Seoul. Now that my flight to Tokyo is delayed, I'm going to miss my connection, and I need to rebook my flight from Narita to Incheon."

The customer that Glen waved over paused behind the young man and returned to the front of the line.

"There are other customers in this same predicament, sir."

"Then why won't you do anything?"

"Because rebooking is the responsibility of the employees at the gate. If you could just be a little more patient, you will be able to rebook there."

"Listen. I already took time off work to come here on short notice. Getting here was a huge pain in the ass, and I don't want to have to miss any more time than I need to."

"Well, I'm sorry sir, but there's nothing I can do." Glen grew giddy as he uttered the phrase.

The young man threw his arms up and walked away. While that bit of drama at the end of the conversation had pleased Glen, he wished that the customer had been more upset. People flying to other parts of the world were generally angrier than this man had been, mostly because delays created a domino effect of complications more easily.

When Glen and Scott were both free of customers, Glen turned to his friend and said, "Hey man, do you want to head over to Facades once we get off? Get some Redbull vodkas and maybe sweet talk some layover divorcees? Let's swoop some babes."

Scott tilted his head back and said, "Facades? That's too far of a walk from here."

"So what? Facades always has the best honeys, and you know it."

"That's true."

"I'm gonna cram someone good tonight. Can't wait to get my dick wet."

Teresa, having overheard her coworkers, finished telling a passenger that they would have to keep the middle seat despite having reserved the window seat and chimed in with, "You can't talk like that."

"Shut your bird lips, Teresa," Glen said. "You don't know anything about anything."

"I know that the way you talk about 'swooping babes' at an airport bar makes me uncomfortable."

Scott leaned back in his chair so that Glen and Teresa could make eye contact.

Glen scoffed. "'Uncomfortable.' You don't even know how I operate. I'm cerebral with my approach," he said as he shrugged his shoulders.

"No you aren't," Teresa said. Scott raised his eyebrows.

Before Glen could drum up a retort, the young man from earlier stormed up to him and slammed his hand on the counter.

The loud smack of the index finger ring made Glen jump in his seat, and he said, "Sir, I'm going to have to ask you to calm down."

"Dude, I was just thinking about how you handled my situation, and I couldn't leave it there. I live in Seoul, and just flew all the way here so that I could go to my ex-girlfriend's wedding uninvited. It was extremely embarrassing, and I'm embarrassed to be telling you now, but can you please find a way to help me out?"

"Wedding crasher! That's dope, man. You're an international Vince Vaughn," Scott said.

"Or Owen Wilson," Glen added.

"Shut up," the customer said to both of them. "My first ever visit to Chicago has been the shittiest experience of my life, and all I want to do is get back to my daily routine before I lose my mind. Can you please, please, please get me on a flight as soon as possible?"

Glen reflected on the situation and said, "I'm sorry for your trouble sir, but there's just nothing I can do. Rebooking flights is out of my power. You will have to go to the gate."

The young man scoffed and said, "What do you even do here?"

"Excuse me?" Glen responded.

"This desk claims to be where customers get served, but you're not making any kind of effort to serve me. You didn't even look at the computer before you told me that you couldn't do anything."

"It's company policy, sir," Glen said as he pretended to look up the man's itinerary. He was actually looking at Facebook.

"The company policy is to disrespect customers by not even making an effort to help them?"

"Okay, sir. I'll find a flight for you."

The customer let out a sigh of relief and said, "Really? That'd be great."

Glen looked at the itineraries and saw that he could book a direct flight to Seoul with Asiana Airlines the next morning, but decided that wasn't good enough. He found an itinerary he liked.

"Here we go," he said, holding back a smile. "This Singapore Airlines itinerary will take you to San Francisco tomorrow at 2:15 P.M."

"You don't have any direct flights tomorrow?"

"Please, sir, let me finish. You'll have a seven-hour layover in San Francisco before flying to Hong Kong. You'll do a quick switch there and go to Singapore before arriving in Seoul on Thursday at 10 P.M. local time."

The passenger looked down and shook his head.

"This is the best I can do, sir. If you would like to book this itinerary, I'll have to ask that you pay an additional two thousand thirty-six dollars and sixteen cents. Would that be in credit?"

"I'll just wait for the agents to arrive at the gate."

Glen feigned empathy and said, "I am terribly sorry for your misfortune and any inconvenience you may have suffered. Here is a voucher that will allow you to eat at any restaurant in the airport. The cash value is fifteen dollars." Glen attempted to hand the voucher to the passenger, who, instead of accepting it, stared into his eyes.

"Thanks for nothing," the passenger said before storming off.

"Cry me a river, dick cheese," Glen muttered.

"Some people are so entitled," Scott said.

"Got that right," Glen said. The two employees smacked each other's hands under the counter. "*Ehh, I have to get back to Seoul because Chicago is a peasant city and just being here makes my skin crawl,*" he said, mocking the passenger. "The nerve of that guy. We get it, bro, you travel all over the world. Big deal. Not my fault if your flight is delayed."

Scott grinned and said, "Got that right. So Glen, when's the last time you picked up a chick at Facades?"

"Funny you should ask, because it was just a couple of weeks ago," Glen said. "This coug' was posted up at the bar, sipping a 'mosa. I used that as a convo piece, because it wasn't in the morning, and drinking a 'mosa after brunch is something I notice. She was waiting to fly out to LAX, and was drinking because of her fear of flying. I gave her a drink voucher, and we hit it off. I offered to rebook her flight for her so that she could stay longer, and used more vouchers to get her shit-faced beyond oblivion. Then we headed over to the Sheraton and plowed."

"That's dope," Scott said, nodding his head.

"If that happened, which it didn't, then it would be rapey," Teresa said.

"Um, it did happen, and it was baller," Glen said.

Teresa said, "You make me sick." She looked away from Glen and out at the concourse, shaking her head. The Seoul passenger was standing aimlessly in the middle of the terminal.

Teresa got out of her seat and walked toward him. Glen watched them talk for a moment before they walked away.

"I wonder where they're going," Scott said.

"She's probably going to pity bang him in the janitor's closet," Glen said.

The two employees pounded fists and proceeded to rate the asses of passengers that walked by, using a ten-point scale. They alternated between this activity and disappointing customers for an hour, as there was no sign of Teresa. They did, in this time, get word that all connecting flights from Tokyo Narita would get automatically rebooked after the delayed flight to Tokyo had taken off from O'Hare. Upon hearing this news, Glen and Scott decided that that was the end of the saga with the passenger Glen had begun exclusively referring to as "entitled prick."

When Teresa came back to the Customer Service Desk, she was all smiles. Glen and Scott were more convinced than ever that she had been having sex with the passenger.

"Well look at that grin," Scott said as Teresa sat down in her chair.

"Where were you?" Glen asked. "Banging out?"

"Is that the only possible way that I could make a customer happy?" Teresa said.

"Yeah," Glen said.

"One hundred percent," Scott said.

"Get your heads out of the gutter," Teresa said. "I'm not sure if you know what empathy is, but I didn't want that guy to have to wait around in limbo for his flight to get rebooked. So I went over to his gate and rebooked his connection for him. I got him on a direct flight to Incheon tomorrow and hooked him up with a free hotel room for the night. I thought the lengths he went to were oddly romantic, that meeting his ex-girlfriend's family must have been mortifying. I can't blame him for wanting to get out of here as quickly as possible."

"Where's Incheon?" Scott asked.

"It's where Seoul's airport is," Teresa said.

"Damn dude, you're worthless," Glen said.

"Pretty sure you're the one who's worthless," Teresa said. "That passenger needed help after trying to make a grand gesture, and you just tossed him out like trash."

"So?" Glen said.

"You've gotta help the passengers sometimes," Teresa said.

"You're still too green," Glen said, twiddling a pen. "You don't get it yet."

"Maybe I just don't like working with you. I want to help people," Teresa retorted.

"Do you know the value of what you just gave that limp-dick, because you felt bad for him?" Glen said. "Think about it: You got him a direct flight without even knowing what the plan for rebooking and accommodation for the rest of the passengers was yet. Not only that, but United rebooked all of the connecting flights while you were gone, so you probably just made the company pay extra when you could have just waited it out. You blew a bunch of the company's money without even thinking twice, and you exhibited extreme favoritism. Was this guy a frequent flyer with us?"

Teresa rolled her eyes and said, "No, he didn't mention that he was."

"Then you just did all of this for a regular ol' slapdick passenger. Hope you're feeling good about yourself, Mother Teresa, because that's the kind of shit that gets you fired."

"Dude, you're the man," Scott said.

"Shut up, Scott," Teresa said.

"Don't tell Scott to shut up," Glen said. "Heads up, by the way — you will probably have to answer for what you just did. It didn't follow company protocol at all."

"But I did the right thing," Teresa said, rubbing her elbows. "And I think you're the one who's going to have to answer for what you did."

"What are you talking about? Go work for UNICEF, dummy," Glen said. "What if this guy was making up this sap story about crashing his ex-girlfriend's wedding just to get us to rebook his flight for free? There's no way for us to know. Even if that story is real, that guy's not a MileagePlus member, so you may have just angered someone who is. We've got to look out for our top customers, and no one else."

The three employees sat in silence for a few moments. Glen's walkie talkie cracked to life, and it told him to come to the administrative office. He left his post and stared Teresa down.

"Well will you look at that," Glen said. "This is where I report you."

"If you say so," Teresa said. Glen expected her to be downtrodden, but she smiled at him.

It made him uncomfortable.

"So did we end up deciding on Facades later?" he said to Scott, trying to deflect attention. "We did," Scott said, trying to give Glen an air-five. Glen did not reciprocate, and Scott ran his hand through the hair on the side of his hair, so as to not mess up the spikes.

Glen arrived in the administrative office, which was a small room with worn white walls.

It could just as easily have been used for storage. Glen's supervisor Darryl sat at a desk in the middle of the room. Darryl was an imposing man, with a squarish bald head and shoulders broader than most, but he was well-liked by all of the airline employees. He generally sided with them on all customer issues, which might have been the reason customers were generally not satisfied with their travel experience. He stood up to greet Glen.

Glen shook Darryl's hand. "To what do I owe the pleasure?" he said with a smile. "I hate to say it Glen, but this is no laughing matter," Darryl said as he sat.

"Is there a problem?" Glen said as he sat in turn.

"I don't know how to put this, so I'll just say it. We've been getting complaints about you lately, and this time I have to act. If I don't, it's my ass."

"What, customer complaints? You know that's never an issue. Just sweep their problems under the rug, like always."

"I wish I could, but it's employee complaints. There have been accusations of sexual harassment."

Glen grew restless, but did his best to conceal his feelings. "Really? If I've offended anyone, I apologize."

Darryl said, "You know we have to take these accusations seriously."

"Of course you do," Glen said. "You of all people should know that I respect women more than anyone."

"I know you do your job well, and we're going to try to get to the bottom of this," Darryl said. He looked at the paper on his desk and said, "It's been reported that you routinely talk in-depth about sexual conquests you claim to have made, and you use phrases such as, 'get my dick wet,' 'cram,' 'plow,' and 'pound,' on a regular basis. It also says here that you rate the quality of the buttocks of passersby during almost every shift you work. All of these actions make coworkers and customers uncomfortable. Part of my job is to make sure that everyone who works for us is comfortable, and if I don't address these accusations, the reports will just go higher up."

"Is there any proof to support these accusations, or will you be taking the word of whoever is saying this stuff?"

"Like I said, Glen, no matter how good I think you are at your job, I have to take claims made by my employees seriously."

Glen's face grew red. "It's totally Teresa. She's just pissed that I won't have sex with her. If anything, she's the one that's been sexually harassing me."

Darryl sighed and said, "These are the type of comments that I'm talking about. I'm afraid we're going to have to suspend you without pay and put you through sexual harassment training."

"Darryl, you can't do this to me. I'm the best employee this airline has got."

Darryl's posture was rigid. He slid a pamphlet to Glen and said, "We are confident that you will get the help that you need and come back stronger than ever."

"But Darryl," Glen said as his eyes welled up. "We're bros. We've been to Hooters together."

Darryl looked down and said, "I know, but this is different. If I don't discipline you and offer you sexual harassment training, then we're looking at a lawsuit."

"I'm not going to be able to make rent."

"I'm sorry. Maybe you can do some part-time work on the side to make up the difference. Or stay with family or a friend until you get yourself right."

"Can I stay with you?"

"Glen, that would be a conflict of interest, and you know it."

Glen started to cry. He never imagined that in his career as a customer service representative that he would feel so powerless. "You have to find a way to fire her," he managed to say between sobs.

"That would make us look even worse than ignoring the issue," Darryl said. "Just go to the training and everything will go back to normal."

But Glen knew that everything would not go back to normal. Even after finishing the training, he would still be forced to watch himself around Teresa. "Then I quit," he said, surprising himself.

"Very well," Darryl replied with his eyes down. "We're sorry to see you go. Make sure you file the necessary paperwork with HR."

Glen wiped the tears from his eyes, saluted Darryl, and walked out of the office with his head held high. He was convinced that he'd made a principled stand.

Wall Flowers

The Great Wall of China traced the mountain ridge perfectly, aligning itself with all of the natural contours, curves, and dips of the terrain. The end of the monsoon season had painted the mountains a deep, lush green. It was foggy. Xia, with about a hundred flowers bundled in a large tan pack basket slung over her shoulders, hiked up those mountains to the Mutianyu section of the Wall the same way she did every morning. To keep the flowers from wilting too quickly, she also carried a sheet of ice with her. The fog was not much of an obstacle, as she was used to it shrouding the lower slopes of the mountain. Every time she reached the Wall, the fog was gone. She knew that the Wall, towering over the lowlands, had nothing to do with this dissipation, but she liked to think that the structure had a role in it.

Xia had stopped keeping track of how long she'd been selling flowers at the Wall. She was a fixture there. By now, her appearance was a strong indication of what her activities had been. She walked with a distinct hunch, her chest growing increasingly parallel to the ground with age, and had to crane her neck upwards in order to look at customers through rogue white hairs. Most people she encountered probably wondered how an old woman like her was able to carry that load of hers all the way up the mountain, but the simple truth of it was that repetition led to Xia being able to perform a seemingly arduous task with ease.

Xia knew all of the footholds to aim for and the slippery stones to avoid when hiking up the mountain. The tour groups were generally slow to find their footing, so Xia often crept past them. Steeper inclines notified hikers that the Wall was near, and the end of the trail was marked with a staircase leading up to the ancient structure. By now a cold trickle of the melted ice would always work its way down the back of Xia's floral patterned shirt. Once she finally reached the base of the Wall, with beads of sweat accumulated on her brow like spilled marbles on a floor, she turned to the left. That was the best spot to catch the intersection of tourists from different tour groups, it being near both the staircase that she had just ascended and the dropping off point for the tourists who had forgone the hike to take the cable car. Xia never took the easy way up the mountain because paying for the ride would eat into her profits. Every morning, however, she had to pass the Tsingtao lady, who sold Tsingtao beer out of a cooler cart at a marked up price to tourists and was relentless in her pursuit to get Xia to buy a beer from her.

The Tsingtao lady saw her, and her eyes contracted into slits of eyelash. "Hey, flower granny!" she said. "You look sweaty. Want a beer? Fifty yuan!"

"No, thank you," Xia said, trying to remain as polite as possible. This type of refusal was the best course of action, because revealing the fact that she hadn't had a sip of alcohol in fifty-five years would only serve to elicit a series of pestering questions.

"Come on, I know you're tired from hiking all the way up here. I'll sell it to you for forty," the Tsingtao lady said with a mocking grin.

"That's okay," Xia said. "Have a nice day."

The Tsingtao lady's facial muscles relaxed into a look of contempt. "It doesn't look like you have much longer to live, old lady. You should enjoy yourself."

You should enjoy yourself. Her boyfriend Yong had uttered the same phrase to her decades ago, when she initially refused to try baijiu. Wanting to please him, she eventually relented and allowed him to pour her a glass. When she took that first sip, her face flushed with warmth, and he greeted her with an expectant smile. Looking into his eyes, she knew that she had a new favorite pastime.

Xia tried to shake herself free of the memory and continued on to the spot at which she liked to sell her flowers. She hated the Tsingtao lady for always trying to get her to cave in, and for going about it so shamelessly. Xia didn't want to drink any beer, and nothing was going to change that. Not only did she think that a sober flower granny would sell more than a drunk one, but she thought that alcohol only brought out the worst in her. She'd lost too many people close to her because of the drink — most notably Yong. Knowing the reason for her him walking out on her was easy for the most part; it was because he didn't want to come home from work every night to a drunken wife who hadn't even bothered to make a dish as simple as scallion pancakes. The relationship had ultimately fractured once and for all one night when Xia was in a drunken stupor from drinking too much baijiu. Her head still throbbed sometimes when she tried to recall what she'd said and done, even fifty-five years later. What she would give to remember the way everything transpired.

Xia always thought it best to continue moving when she sold her flowers. Of the tourists she ran into, couples were most likely to buy her roses, carnations, daffodils, and lilies. Of those couples, the ones she approached immediately after they had taken in a particularly majestic vista were the most likely to buy. Xia was careful not to interrupt their enjoyment of the view, unlike some of the other flower grannies she'd see when went into Beijing every so often.

Those women went right up to people and stuck flowers in their faces while they were eating at restaurants. Xia learned from experience that that didn't work with people, especially Western tourists.

She checked her fanny pack for the change necessary to make cash transactions. A nice distribution of small and large bills, plus coins, was present. The last thing she wanted was to be unable to make a sale due to her not having the proper change. She took a deep breath and ascended the final set of steps that took her to the top of the Wall.

The tourists flowed on and off the Wall at a steady rate. Multiple languages filled the air, and despite her working here for so long, they were indecipherable. Xia guessed that she heard German, Russian, and Spanish, but they could just as easily have been been Dutch, Polish, and Italian. She knew that English was used often, but didn't know anything beyond the most basic phrases. Of course, fewer than half of the tourists so much as made eye contact with her, and of that fraction, none of them indicated any interest in buying flowers. All they cared about was the Wall. To be fair to the tourists, though, Xia's opinion regarding the Wall was that it was the greatest sight that anyone could ever lay eyes on. There was no way that other famous landmarks around the world represented the persever- ance and unifying power of national pride that the Wall did. As Chairman Mao once said, "He who has not been to the Great Wall is not a true man." Xia wholeheartedly believed this, and she considered it a privilege to be able to see such an amazing structure up close every single day. Another joy that Xia derived from her work was seeing the looks on people's faces when they arrived at the Wall for the first time. She envied them, because no feeling was greater than one's first encounter with it.

As she proceeded along the Wall, Xia allowed its majesty to breathe optimism into her. Even with the ever-shrinking block of ice doing little to prevent her flowers from wilting under the summer sun, she felt that she would sell enough to meet her quota. It wasn't like doing so mattered much these days. She only had to provide for herself, and the expenses required for that were dwindling with time. After she quit drinking, she had never been an indulgent woman. The reason she sold flowers in the first place was because she didn't have enough money to support herself after she retired from the shoe factory outside of Beijing. She'd worked on the assembly line for thirty years and couldn't say that it was a gratifying job, but she tolerated it because her mother had beat it into her head that she was lucky to be working in the first place, spinster that she was. Even though it involved a hike every day, selling flowers was a more relaxing job.

Finally, a lone tourist walked toward her. He wore a gray tank top that revealed pale arms, and his hands were tucked into the pockets of his black basketball shorts. What stood out to Xia most, however, was that he walked with his head down. Everyone else kept their eyes up to look at the Wall and the surrounding scenery. She sensed that this indifference was presenting her with an opportunity.

"Young man," she said as he got within earshot, hoping that his inability to understand Mandarin wouldn't be a factor in grabbing his attention.

He ignored her.

When the young man got close enough to touch, she tried to stop him by placing her hand on his clammy shoulder.

He drew back, startled.

She pulled a bouquet of red carnations from her collection with the deftness of an archer pulling an arrow from a quiver. She presented the flowers to him. "For your girlfriend," she said in the best English that she could muster.

He put his hand up at about the same level as her face and shook it in unison with his head.

She knew that he was refusing her, but did not want to take no for an answer. She felt that the Wall wanted her to make this sale.

The young man continued to shake his head as he walked past her.

For the next hour, the crowd grew. Xia made a few sales, but the remaining flowers started to wilt. She'd considered bringing a cooler with her, as the Tsingtao lady had for her beers, but this was out of the question. Carrying the flowers and sheet of ice was routine, but adding a cooler to the equation was too wearisome of an obstacle to overcome. As the sun rose higher in the blue sky, Xia descended from the Wall because there was a boulder near the Tsingtao lady that she liked to sit on and sell flowers from when she got tired.

She pulled the pack basket off and set the flowers on the ground. By now the sheet of ice was completely melted. Half of the basket was dyed mahogany by the melted ice, and water dripped from the bottom of it. A dark stream ran down her rounded back. The Tsingtao lady noticed that she was exhausted.

"Hey flower granny," she called over.

Xia tried to ignore her, but a slight grimace betrayed the fact that she'd heard.

"Why don't you just come over here and have a Tsingtao? You'd be crazy to refuse on a day like this."

Xia flicked her hand at her.

"You'll see," the Tsingtao lady said.

From that spot, Xia was able to make a couple more sales. Every time a tourist bought flowers from her, she smiled as brightly as she could, hoping that they wouldn't notice the gap where her incisor should have been. She carried on like this for twenty minutes before she saw the young Western man again. With his tank top a significantly darker gray than when he had first come by, the tourist stormed past Xia. He was as determined to get a Tsingtao as he would be to reach an oasis in the Gobi. Xia tried feebly to offer him a lily, but was too slow to pull the flower back to her chest before he walked straight through it. With her grip as weak as it was, the flower fell meekly to the ground, where it was promptly smashed by the tourist's New Balance sneaker. He flipped a dismissive hand up in the air, casting Xia's concerns aside and ordering a beer with one gesture.

Xia bent over to pick up the crumpled flower, not be-lieving that her product should ever be left on the ground like that. Before she could stand back up, she felt a stabbing pain in her lower back. The sharpness of it reminded her of that blow to the head with a bottle of baijiu on that fateful night ages prior. The bottle didn't break, but the clear liquor spilled onto her face as she fell to the ground. With her eyes burning, she'd watched Yong leave her behind, forever.

Lying on the ground was a much more comfortable pros-pect than standing, so that is what Xia did. The relief was marginal at best, as she was in complete and utter anguish. For the next five minutes, she lay on the ground, doing her best to suppress the moans of pain seeping out of her mouth. Meanwhile, the Tsingtao lady continued with her standard marketing strategy of carrying on small talk with prospective customers. She didn't speak with the young man in the gray tank top, however, as he sat alone at a table away from her cart. He forlornly sipped his giant green beer bottle as he looked at his phone. This bothered Xia. It was one thing if the young man refrained from helping her because he was too busy soaking up inspiration from the Wall, but she thought ignoring an old lady in pain in order to look at his phone was inexcusable.

After the young man finished his beer, he walked toward Xia. He held his phone in front of him, staring at it as if it contained all of the answers of the universe. Perhaps he was preparing his camera so that he could take a picture of the Wall after all. Xia knew this was her last chance to sell her flowers to him.

Before the tourist reached her, she propped herself up so that she could lean on the boulder. He'd been curt earlier, so this would require effort. Once the young man got within reach, she jutted a bouquet of tulips out with all of her might. This surprised the tourist, who dropped his phone. Embarrassed, she reached for it, thinking that returning it would mollify him. Before the now-angered man ripped the phone from her grasp, she saw a photo of a blonde woman in a wedding dress. The young bride smiled radiantly, with her dimples plainly visible in the small image. She was with her groom as well, and despite the fact that Xia hadn't gotten a good look at him, she knew that he was not the young man before her. The tourist had been looking at pictures of a woman marrying someone else.

Remembering what it felt like when she'd heard that Yong had married another woman, and all of the regret and envy that went along with it, she wished more than ever that she could speak English. If only she could warn this young man against wallowing in absolute sadness, the kind that makes one hole themselves up in their room for days on end and question the reason that they are even alive at all, she'd be able to help him. If only she could prevent him from falling headlong into the same depressing cycle that she had, he'd move on with his life. Seeing that the young man's brown eyes had welled up, she thought that there was only one possible solution.

She presented the bouquet of tulips to the foreigner once again, but much more gently and with her head lowered. In order to prevent him from misunderstanding her, she shouted, "Free! Free! Free!" The last thing she wanted at this point was for him to think that she was trying to take advantage of his fragile emotional state.

The young man rapidly and repeatedly pulled the front of his tank top out so as to cool himself down with his own personal breeze. He bowed his head and took the flowers. He said, "Thank you," as he fumbled with the flowers. Before Xia could present him with a smile, he turned away from her and hurled the bouquet up and over the Wall. The flowers went end over end, with a few rogue petals peeling off and fluttering listlessly down onto the elevated walkway. The young man skulked off, leaving Xia in the wake of his anger and frustration.

She thought about why he would go so far as to throw her offering over the Wall, and while she considered this, and the bouquet going end over end, she suddenly remembered why she'd been hit in the head with the bottle of baijiu and lost Yong forever.

That night, she'd been enjoying drinks with him in a local courtyard restaurant decorated with red lanterns strung above the tables. She remembered that she could see the stars, which was never the case in Beijing anymore. As she recalled, another woman approached the table.

Yong awkwardly grabbed the woman's hand. He and the stranger smiled at each other before turning their gaze to Xia.

"Xia, I'd like you to meet my betrothed."

"What are you talking about?" Xia slurred.

"This is who I plan on marrying. I'm sorry."

The first words to come out of Xia's mouth were, "Are you trying to steal my husband?"

"What?" the woman replied.

"You're jealous of me, so you had to come in and steal him?"

"Our mothers introduced us," the woman said as Yong twiddled his fingers. "We're a perfect match."

"You and I aren't married, Xia," Yong said. He looked down and added, "Mother likes that she doesn't drink too much."

The courtyard spun, with the lanterns coalescing into one uniform blur, but Xia wasn't sure if it was because of the news or the baijiu. She pointed at the woman and yelled, "You couldn't stand the sight of me living a happy life with the perfect man for me, while you rotted away as a spinster. So you made eyes at him and he fell for it, you whore!"

"I don't even know you."

"You had to know that I couldn't go against the word of my parents, Xia. This is the only way I could tell you how I feel without you losing control."

"Losing control?"

"That's what he said," the woman confirmed. Xia leapt up and grabbed the woman's hair.

That was when the bottle came crashing down on her head. The next image that came back to her was Yong growling in frustration and throwing the baijiu bottle over the courtyard walls. It sailed end over end.

Tears came to her eyes and burst through like water through a broken dam. They filled the deep rivets in her cheeks the way floodwaters fill a dry riverbank. The clarity with which she recalled that night made her feel an overwhelming sense of revulsion. She didn't know what to do. Maybe she could go home and curl up on her bed. The Wall was not the place for her to be — it was far too dignified. In her eyes, it was certain that the people who came there wanted to see something truly magnificent, and she certainly did not feel that she fit the description.

Suddenly every passerby seemed to gawk at her and wonder why such a hunchbacked monstrosity would have the audacity to peddle her flowers near the most astounding man-made structure in the world.

Ignoring her back pain, she gathered up all of her flowers and strapped on her pack basket before leaving the Wall once and for all. At this point, she didn't care about spending money on a cable car ticket — between the physical and mental pain, she simply needed to get out. Before she could make her way over to the embarkation point, however, the Tsingtao lady called to her one last time.

"Hey, granny! You look like you need a drink!"

After initially thinking that she should continue walking, Xia stopped and said, "Okay," before using her sleeve to wipe the tears off her cheek.

"Really?!" the Tsingtao lady replied with a cackle. "I never thought that this day would come." She grabbed the bottle as quickly as she could, and even though she ordinarily handed a bottle opener to her customers so that they'd open the bottle themselves, she did the deed for Xia.

Upon seeing the giant bottle of beer thrust in her face, Xia slipped the straps off and dropped the flowers on the ground. For the first time in ages, she felt free. The bottle was icy cold to the touch, which not only startled her, but allowed her to realize that a cold Tsingtao was indeed perfect for tourists who had hiked up the mountain, walked the steps along the top of the Wall, or both.

"Free of charge. You saying yes to a beer is enough for me," the Tsingtao lady said with a smile that Xia usually thought of as menacing, but now saw as accommodating.

"I need to enjoy myself, right?" Xia said.

The Tsingtao lady laughed. "That's right," she replied. She gestured toward the eating area between her cart and Xia's resting boulder.

"Thank you," Xia replied, ignoring the gesture. With her fingers already growing numb from the cold, wet bottle, she proceeded to the Wall. Her flowers lay sideways on the ground, spilled out of the pack basket.

Beer bottle in hand, Xia returned to the top of the Wall. Her legs burned beyond belief, but the prospect of the view she'd have forced her on. When she made it up there, it felt like it was her first time. For the first time in longer than she could remember, she truly saw the vast, rolling forest beyond the Wall. It was a completely different world up here. She brought the bottle to her lips and took a swig of the beer. The carbonation caught her off guard, as it was more bubbly than she'd remembered. The same warmth that came to her face the first time she tried baijiu returned, and she laughed. She didn't need Yong, her flowers, or the approval of tourists. All she needed was the Wall.

A Bridge Abridged

Despite looking exactly the same, San Clemente seemed infinitely more boring than Sean had remembered it. It wasn't that anything changed to make it more boring — such as opening a bunch of antique shops along Avenida Del Mar — but rather the fact that nothing was different. Families and tourists still ambled along the entrance to the beach, stopping off at the snack bar for ice cream. Surfers rinsed off under the showerheads underneath The Fisherman's Restaurant, and fit couples walked their German shepherds on the beach path that ran alongside the railroad tracks.

Everything was just as aimless as Sean remembered. He couldn't figure out exactly what it was that he had wanted to see changed or why San Clemente's stasis bothered him, but the feeling that he had was akin to stepping out of a time machine three years into the past. He found it unsettling. Before he moved to Korea, the white houses dotting the coastal hills had instilled a Mediterranean aesthetic that he was proud of. Now he thought that the houses were kitschy. He thought it looked like an imitation Amalfi, and he didn't like it. The expressions of the beachgoers betrayed the fact that they adored the sleepy beach town for what it was, but now Sean could only see it as tired.

Seeing high school kids swimming and flirting on the beach as he had in the past reminded him that his teenage years did not resemble the romanticized image he had once crafted for himself. He now thought that there was nothing cool about frolicking on the beach. After passing a group of teenagers congregating around a fire pit and noticing a young couple among the group wearing hoodies and loosely holding hands, Sean decided it was time to end his walk. He'd be expected at The Fisherman's for an early dinner, anyway, so it was a good time to turn back.

Since the restaurant comprised two buildings straddling the base of the pier, Sean caught a glimpse of the pier as he arrived at the restaurant. It was the same as always — the restaurant supported by stilts served as a gateway to the ocean. The American flag flew over it. Sean peered down the lengthy path beyond the shore and thought about extending his stroll. It stretched toward the horizon, with the occasional lifeguard tower and snack shop flanking it. He couldn't see the end clearly, but he guessed that there were people fishing off it. There always were three years ago, and Sean didn't figure that people's fishing habits would be the only thing about San Clemente that had changed. Deciding to forego the pier, he grabbed the handle of the door, which was sticky with dried saltwater, and entered the restaurant. He worked his way through the restaurant, as he had done hundreds of times before, and noted the sailor's pub aesthetic the restaurant was going for. He appreciated that there were at least people who fished in San Clemente, but doubted that it was ever a fishing hub. A fish was mounted above one of the windows, but that didn't necessarily mean it was caught by anyone from San Clemente. Sean walked past the fish and out onto the patio, where tables sat under blue umbrellas.

When Sean found his party's table, his dad Sam and brother Sid were already seated. He approached the table.

"Where'd you go, bud?" Sam said. "We thought you went off to Asia again."

Sid pulled out his phone and started looking at it.

"I wanted to see the beach, so I took a walk," Sean said without faking a laugh.

"Okay. Did you see anything you liked?"

"A lot of the same old stuff," Sean said as he put his napkin on his lap. "I can't wait to eat the scallops."

Sid continued to look at his phone.

"They're still amazing," his dad said, as he opened his menu.

The server came by, dressed in all black. He said, "Are we thinking of drink orders yet?"

"I'll have a Bud Light, please," Sam said.

After a moment of the server waiting for him, Sid looked up from his phone and said, "Pacifico."

The server wrote these orders down, turned to Sean, and said, "And for you, sir?"

"Could I get a gin and tonic?"

The server said he could, told them he'd get the drinks, and left them. "Since when did you start drinking gin and tonics?" Sam said.

"Probably my first year in Korea," Sean said. "There's this bar in Gangnam where you pay twenty bucks at the door then get unlimited cocktails for free."

By the time Sean had finished the sentence, Sam was looking at the menu again. He looked up at Sean and said, "What do you think of splitting some oysters?"

At that moment, Sean's friends Ricky and Martin arrived. Sean hadn't seen either of them in person for the past three years. All of their conversations had taken place over Skype and social media, which left Sean unsure of how to act around them. It was the first time that seeing them made him nervous since he'd arrived at Martin's house for the sleepover in third grade that solidified his position in their crew. Once he'd known his standing with them was firm, Sean took to teasing Ricky and Martin by calling them "La Vida Loca." Ricky and Martin had always claimed that the jab was a bit of a stretch, but Sean thought it'd been hilarious.

When Sean saw the two of them, he said, "Hey, guys!" He didn't want to use the old nickname and open up the nostalgia gates.

Ricky and Martin roared at the sight of him, excited to see their friend after all of this time, and Sean felt his initial anxiety fade away. These were his best friends. He hugged both of them, then they all traded pleasantries and sat down. Sam made them pose for a couple of pictures, which Sean hated, with the ocean in the background. He was of the opinion that posing forced the moment, whereas candid pictures captured the true essence. There was no better way to kill a party than to have people pose for pictures.

After he'd been appeased, Sam suggested that everyone look at their menus, because the server would be back.

"I've got loads of stories to tell you guys," Sean said.

"I bet," Ricky said.

"I'm sure," Martin added. "But first, we wanted to talk about something that came up this week."

"Yeah," Ricky said.

"Okay," Sean said, twiddling his fingers.

Before they could start, the server returned with the drinks. He took drink orders from Ricky and Martin, and appetizer orders for the table. Sam ordered Oysters Rockefeller. After the server left, everyone toasted to Sean's return. Ricky and Martin mimed their clinking.

After the toast, Martin said, "Remember the time we TP'd Mr. Lawson's house and almost got caught? And then the next Monday in class he mentioned it and we had to stop ourselves from laughing?"

Ricky said, "How awesome was that?"

Sean said, "So that was the thing that came up this week?"

"Yup."

Sean indulged him with a fake laugh. High school stories about toilet-papering the teacher's house are not very exciting when you've been to the jungle.

"I think he knew it was us, but he didn't have the proof," Martin said.

"Absolutely," Ricky said.

A moment passed while Sean took a swig of his gin and tonic. He then said, "So when I went to Australia, I drove on a road that was pretty much exactly like the PCH."

"Dude, really?" Martin said.

"Yeah. It might've actually been better. It was called The Great Ocean Ro—"

Ricky chimed in with, "The PCH is so gnarly, dude. Sean, do you remember that time we went up to SF, and you had to take a shit, so we pulled over right on the side of the road and you did it?"

Martin burst into laughter. "Bro, that was hilarious."

"Was it?" Sean said, his expression dead serious.

"Yeah, man," Ricky said. "That was always your favorite story."

"It was," Sean said as Martin looked on. Sean decided that being straightforward was better, so he added, "But I'm not really interested in reliving high school anymore, guys. I want to hear about what you guys have been up to these days."

"We've been having a blast, dude," Martin said. "Last week, we went up to The Trifecta every night. Ole's is still the best bar up there."

Ole's was the bar that they'd always gone to when they were home from college. "Nobody there can beat me at pool," Sam said.

"Yeah right," Martin said. "I'm a regular shark these days."

"If by shark you mean sucker, then I guess so," Ricky said. "But you're right about Ole's being the best bar," he continued. "And it's still easy to tell who the tourists are, because they're even worse at pool than you are."

The server brought Ricky and Martin their beers. They'd both ordered Lagunitas IPAs.

After taking another swig of gin and tonic, Sean said, "You know in Korea they have self-serve bars, where you just take the bottles from a refrigerator, collect the empties in a basket on the table, and pay at the end?"

Martin, drawing his beer away from his lips, said, "Dude, Ole's has been getting a lot of tourists lately. It bums me out because they're lame. I'm actually cool with it, though, because I look a lot better at pool when I play them. Helps out with the pursuit."

Sean rubbed his temple and said, "Is there anything you guys have been doing that's new? Like, not the same stuff we always did?" He'd accented it more sharply than he wanted, and knew instantly that Ricky and Martin had picked up on his tone.

Ricky said, "First off, Ole's is the spot. Don't you remember how dope it was in high school, when we had fake IDs?"

"You guys had fake IDs?" Sam said.

"You've got to move on, guys. That stuff is lame," Sean said with a flick of the wrist.

Martin tapped Ricky on the shoulder and said, "I see what's going on here, Ricky. We've never been to Korea, or Australia, or wherever else Sean has been, so we're not cool enough anymore."

The rest of the meal was cloaked in an awkwardness the trio had never experienced before. Sam tried to bridge the gap with small talk, but nobody really engaged him. Throughout it all, Sid stayed on his phone. As a result, Ricky and Martin left after dinner. They said they were going home, but Sean suspected they were going to Ole's.

After they arrived at home, Sean went into the living room with Sid, and Sam went into his bedroom. Sean was upset over what he saw as his friends' closed-mindedness. He sat on the couch with his brother.

"Hey bro," Sean said, holding a pillow to his chest like a toddler might clutch a doll.

"Sup," Sid said without looking up.

"Did I ever tell you about Allie?" he asked. Allie had never been too nostalgic, which was part of why he had been so drawn to her in the first place.

"I saw pictures of her on Facebook," Sid said. "Things seemed pretty serious for awhile there."

"They were," Sean said. "We traveled everywhere together, and we even talked about her moving here after finishing up in Korea. She was perfect for me, but I blew it."

"Okay," Sid said while browsing Tinder.

"It's kind of a bummer," Sean said.

"Why are you telling me this?" Sid asked, finally looking him in the eye. "If you want me to tell you to go and get her back, then just do it already."

"I can't," Sean said, averting his eyes.

"Why not?" his brother said, looking at his phone. The sun was beginning its descent into the ocean, and the orange light slid through the windows.

Sean sighed. "This one time, when we were in Bangkok, I had sex with a hooker. I told her about it a few days later in

Myanmar. She packed her things right when she got back to Korea and moved back to Chicago. Pulled a midnight run and disappeared without telling her school."

"Why didn't you quit, too?"

"I couldn't. I'd just renewed my contract at my school, and if I broke early I wouldn't get my severance or pension." Sean's face was red. Not from embarrassment, but from the dying sunlight.

"She'll probably get over it, man. Chicks always get over things after a while."

"She'll never forgive me for it."

"How do you know?"

"She's married now."

"What an idiot."

"Thanks, man. I've always thought that I was in the wrong, but it's nice to know someone is on my side."

Sid looked up from his phone. "Oh," he said as he scratched his head. "I wasn't saying that she's an idiot for not forgiving you. I was saying that she's an idiot for getting married." The sun was gone.

Feeling lower than he had in months, Sean went into the kitchen. From the couch, Sid commended him for having had sex with someone "exotic."

Sam was in the kitchen when Sean walked in. He stood in front of the refrigerator, holding a Ziploc of cold pizza in his hands. He smiled sheepishly and said, "A little pizza never hurt anyone, right?"

"Whatever you say, Dad."

"Hey bud, I'm sure those guys had a reason for being upset tonight."

"What's that supposed to mean?" Sean asked as he moved past his dad and grabbed a Lagunitas out of the refrigerator.

Sam shrugged and said, "They just wanted to have fun, you know. You didn't have to be so tough on them."

Sean grimaced as he took a swig from the bottle.

"You'll see them soon though, right?"

"Yeah," Sean said. "How are Grandpa and Uncle Seb?" he asked, changing the subject to the welfare of his two favorite relatives. "Is Grandpa still playing video games?" Video games had always been a hobby of his grandfather's. Some of Sean's first memories took place right after his mother had left the family, and consisted of the two of them staying up late into the night to play Super Mario 3 together. Sean had always bragged about his grandfather's affinity for video games to the other kids at school. Nobody else had a grandpa who knew how to do Mortal Kombat fatalities.

"I meant to tell you Sean," Sam said, looking directly into his son's eyes. "Grandpa's been having a rough go of it lately, so Uncle Seb moved in with him. You can call them if you want." Sam clawed into his pocket for his phone.

"Okay," Sean said, extending his hand.

His dad dialed and handed the phone to him, who took a seat at the kitchen table while he waited to hear his grandfather's voice. The remote control sat in his place at the kitchen table, so he picked it up and set it at the place next to his. He wondered why a remote control would be at the kitchen table in the first place. Everything was working to annoy him, but he was sure that his grandfather would stabilize him, as he always had.

"Hey, it's little Sam," Sean's grandpa said upon answering.

"It's Sean, grandpa," Sean asserted. "I'm back from Korea." He waited for his grandfather's excited response. Sam brought Sean a glass of water.

Grandpa said, "Oh is that right? Fighting the commies, were you?" His voice was noticeably weaker, and much hoarser than Sean had recalled. "I was over there, too, you know. You shoot one Chinese, and two of them pop up." Sean could hear Uncle Seb protest in the background.

He raised his eyebrows. "Sure. Is Uncle Seb with you?" He looked at his dad, who was helping himself to another slice of cold pizza. He wouldn't make eye contact with Sean.

"Hey Sean," Uncle Seb said, taking over. "It's great to hear your voice." "Good to hear you, too. Hey, is Grandpa alright?"

An uncomfortable pause followed. "Did you not know?" Uncle Seb asked. Sean scrambled for an answer, but couldn't come up with one.

"You beatniks are all the same," his grandpa bellowed in the background. Sean's dad came over to him, with his eyes affixed to his toes.

Sean put his hand over the phone and said, "Dad." His father didn't look up.

"Why didn't you tell me about Grandpa?" he asked. Sam motioned for Sean to give him the phone, and Sean obliged. Sam told his brother he'd call him back, then sat down next to Sean and said, "This has all happened pretty recently, and I knew you were handling all of your affairs with Korea and everything, so I didn't want to distract you."

Sean struggled to stifle his tears. "A little heads up would've been nice."

"I'm sorry, Sean. We're doing what we can to minimize the effects."

Sean averted his eyes and said, "Like what?"

"Uncle Seb's got him on an organic diet," his dad said, placing a hand on Sean's shoulder. "He gives him spoonfuls of coconut oil every morning, too. That helps, I guess. Dr. Oz did a segment on it or something."

When Sean pictured his grandpa, he saw a man who showed him that the first secret whistle was behind the curtain in the third level of the first world, and that you had to make

Mario duck on a floating white block above the bushes to get back there. Now, he was a shell of what he used to be.

"Can we go visit him sometime soon?" Sean asked.

"Sure," his dad said. "Any time you want."

"Good," Sean said. After another moment, he said, "What do you think mom would have done about this?"

"Who cares," Sam answered, rubbing his hands together. After moment so quiet they could hear Sid's fingernail click on the screen of his phone as he swiped it, Sam said, "So Sean, Have you gotten any companies to call you back yet?"

Sean was still rattled by the development with his grandpa, so it took him a moment to respond. "No, nothing yet," he said.

"You should probably follow up, don't you think?" Sam said as he grabbed the remote and turned on the TV. Fox News showed Donald Trump wearing a red hat at a rally. "It's something you're going to have to handle at some point."

"Yeah," Sean said absent-mindedly. "I'll get on that this week." The truth was that he was too worried about his grandfather to care about anything else, and he was incensed with his father for casually steering the conversation toward his flagging job prospects. Everything about that phone call, from the nonsensical statements to the sound of his grandfather's voice, depressed him.

"How much money did you end up saving while you were in Korea, anyway?" Sean's dad said while settling on an episode of *American Pickers*.

"The severance package and pension are a pretty good deal, so after the car I've got about seven grand."

"You're still going to have to make a down payment on an apartment, so it looks like you're not gonna have much left after that," his dad said, twirling the remote in his hand. "If I had to guess, I'd say that you probably traveled a little bit too much."

Sean's face grew hot and he said, "Part of going over there was to see the world. What was I going to do, just curl up in my studio apartment and not do anything ever?"

"I'm not saying you couldn't have fun. You're young, but you've got to consider the future."

Sean was flabbergasted."What kind of future do I have? Nothing will ever be better than the time I spent living abroad, and look at where that 'adventure' is getting me — nobody wants to hire somebody who has zero experience in the field."

Sam turned his head around halfway to catch a glimpse of Sean out of the corner of his eye. "Just take a look at your brother Sid," he said, flicking his wrist in the direction of the sofa. "He's younger than you are, but he has a steady job in Irvine that allows him to pay rent on a one-bedroom apartment *and* put money away. You've been putzing around, being some kind of worldly traveler or something."

Sean said, "Sorry I've decided to enjoy my life and get more out of it than you have. You just got married young and never went anywhere, and then had to sit back and watch as your son ticked off boxes on your bucket list before you could. No wonder mom left you." He knew instantly that he probably shouldn't have said that.

Sam said, "What the hell did you just say to me?"

"Nothing."

"You know what?" Sam said as he stood up.

"You're afraid of the real world."

"No I'm not," Sean said.

"Yes you are," Sam said. "That's why you felt like you had to run away after college and do this teaching abroad thing. You were too lazy to get a real job, so you decided to live in a fantasy. Now you're behind."

Sean walked to the front door and said, "I'm going for a walk." His dad said, "Good. Maybe you'll find the real world out there."

Too flustered to come up with a response, Sean slipped on his shoes as fast as he could and slammed the door on his way out.

The San Clemente houses Sean had grown bored with had always looked fake, but they looked especially artificial in the night. While listlessly bathing in street lights the way an iguana might bathe in its terrarium light, they looked like they were part of a movie set. Sean ran with it, and started to think of himself as the star of a fabricated story, like the way Jim Carrey was in *The Truman Show*. Too bad he had already driven away the woman who could show him the truth.

Since he was out, Sean decided that he would head over to the bars and see what Ricky and Martin had been hyping up so enthusiastically. It wasn't so much that he wanted to discover anything new, but more that he wanted to affirm his opinion on the town being the same, culturally isolated place that it always had been. In an odd way, as he walked in the streets of San Clemente, he felt less at ease than he had wandering the streets of Beijing the week before.

The fresh, salty air of the sea hit him as he got to the main drag of Avenida Del Mar. He looked up the street to see where he could go, and saw clumps of Baby Boomers. Everyone seemed to have bleached blonde hair, and the ubiquitous white summer linens were reminiscent of cult fashion. As he passed H.H. Cotton's, the bar that typically had too-loud live music on weekends, he imagined that poisoned Kool-Aid was being served inside.

Seeing that the white-linen people would be the crowd he'd be sharing the bars with, Sean decided to turn back. He wanted a drink though, but couldn't get one without going into a bar. In Seoul he used to walk into a 7-Eleven, buy some beer, and walk with it nearly every weekend. This would be more difficult to do in California, however, and he didn't want to run the risk of having a cop see him brown bagging it. Sans beer and a little bit sadder, Sean walked down the street, in the direction of the beach.

Tomorrow the shops would be alive with locals and tourists coming to check out the Sunday market and be amused by all of the beach town trinkets such as keychains, hats, and knockoff sunglasses. Some of them would marvel at the novelty of a candy store, as if they had never seen one anywhere else.

At this hour, however, all of the shops were closed, dormant shells of themselves. All of the knockoff sunglasses, hats, keychains, and candy were safely packed away. The thought of everyone milling around all hunky dory, as if San Clemente were the best place in the world, made Sean sick. Down the hill in the distance, he saw the moon shining on the ocean, and the effect drew him to it like ants to a pineapple cake.

While he made his way down the sloping road, leaning back to balance his stride, Sean thought back on the interactions that had played out with his friends and family earlier, and he felt an enormous weight of disappointment. This was not the way he had planned on coming back to the United States, and, truth be told, he felt more out of place here than he ever remembered feeling in Korea. He wondered why nobody cared about his experiences abroad, and why they only wanted him to slide seamlessly into what they perceived to be a normal life. He wanted them to appreciate the life that he'd led.

The waves crashed on the shore as Sean crossed the railroad tracks and arrived at the beach. The pier lay straight in front of him. The Fisherman's sat where he left it earlier.

Sean could see through the windows that the only people remaining were the locals sitting at the bar, polishing off their beers among upturned chairs sat atop tables. Looking down the pier he thought of it as a bridge back to where he had spent the past three years living, loving, and losing. He saw it as only natural that he would walk the bridge, and get as close to those memories as he could.

Step by step, Sean proceeded down the illuminated pier. To his right, the lights of Dana Point jutted out into the ocean and mocked him like a cruise ship unknowingly passing a castaway. The waves ran soothingly beneath him. It was as if the massive body of water knew that he was coming back to it, and it beckoned in return. He imagined that he was an offering to the ocean, and that it was prepared to be appeased.

Near the end of the pier, Sean pulled his phone out of his pocket. He thought about taking a picture of the moon, but he thought better of it. Instead, Sean went on YouTube and tried to search for "My Night With the Prostitute from Marseilles," by Beirut. It was a song that he'd always listened to with Allie, and it recalled memories of her more vividly than anything else.

As he prepared himself for Zach Condon singing about the aftermath of a one-night tryst, Sean remembered the first time Allie made him listen to Beirut. They were in their hostel in Malaysia, and even though she was upset that they had failed to see wild orangutans, she turned him onto her favorite band. More memories rushed to him. Their walks along the Han River, their fight at a restaurant in Hong Kong, the times they lay in her bed and talked about places they'd like to visit, and the time he'd finally redeemed himself by finding wild koalas for her were all memories that danced through his head. The first time they locked eyes at their initial training session in Gangnam, however, stood out more than any other. He would never forget how vividly green her eyes had appeared, and how he immediately knew that he had to spend time with her. He hadn't even been in Korea for three days, but this was the woman with whom he wanted to share his experience abroad. It wouldn't be until he'd had too much to drink at the karaoke bar later that week that his interest in her was reciprocated, and he'd found the perfect partner to love before inexplicably destroying the relationship in Bangkok.

Sean felt that listening to the song would give him closure, but the page wouldn't load.

He'd forgotten that the signal at the beach, and especially at the end of the pier, was nonexistent. He thought that maybe a text message to Allie would work its way through to her, but then he realized that he didn't even have her phone number. This impediment signaled that he shouldn't be texting her at all, and he put his phone back in his pocket.

All that was left was the Pacific Ocean, glimmering in the moonlight. As Sean looked out at that black mercurial mass, he knew that he had to go back to the other side of it. Either that, or he was going to jump in.

Acknowledgements

Heartfelt thanks to my professors at Chapman University who provided me the with the mentorship and support I needed in order to make this collection happen: Ian Barnard, Jim Blaylock, Richard Bausch, Douglas Cooney, Anna Leahy, Rei Magosaki, Morgan Read-Davidson, Myron Yeager, and my thesis advisor Tom Zoellner. This collection would not have been possible without your guidance. To Joshua Behnken, Kyoko Nakamura, Catherine Le Nguyen, Michelle Rimlinger, Bryan Wisch, and all of my other classmates at Chapman who helped me find myself as a writer. To Andy Rothermich, who took the time to go through the stories and provide me with insightful feedback.

To Jungeun, for being my first reader and greatest supporter. 사랑해.

List of Credits

Some of these stories have appeared elsewhere, in slightly different form: "Noraebang Night Shift" in *Korea Lit*, "Headless Buddha" in *Adelaide Magazine*, "North" in the *Adelaide Literary Awards Anthology 2017*, and "Wall Flowers" in *Adelaide Voices Anthology 2018*.

About the Author

Born in Cleveland, Ohio, Stephen Gallas is an English professor who writes, travels, and studies foreign languages in his spare time. As of the publication of this book, he speaks English, Korean, German, and Mandarin Chinese. After graduating with a BA in Creative Writing from Miami University, he moved to South Korea to teach English. Four years later, Stephen and his wife moved to California, where Stephen got an MFA in Creative Writing at Chapman University. They currently live in Lakewood, Ohio.

Stephen's work has appeared in *Adelaide Magazine, The Los Angeles Review of Books, Korea Lit, Film Daily*, and *Praxis Magazine*. Follow him on Twitter @gallas_s.

www.ingramcontent.com/pod-product-compliance
Lightning Source LLC
Chambersburg PA
CBHW020019030726
47499CB00007B/2184